Bound to Ramble/Bound by Blood

A Seventh Day Duology
Leslie Swartz

Dedication

To Nycole Terpe
You know what you did
Thank you

Playlist

I Hate Myself for Loving You- Liliac (Cover)
I Did Something Bad- Taylor Swift
Don't Blame Me- Taylor Swift
Dancing in the Dark- Jorgen Dahl moe (Cover)
Demons- Imagine Dragons
Dancing With Myself- The Donnas
Love the Way You Lie- Eminem ft. Rihanna
All These Things That I've Done- The Killers
Move Along- All American Rejects
Man of Constant Sorrow- Home Free
Zero- Smashing Pumpkins
Breathe- The Prodigy
No One's Gonna Love You- Band of Horses

BOUND TO RAMBLE

Chapter 1

"I'M AFRAID THE PRICE has gone up since we last spoke," Duncan said, keeping a distance between himself and his buyer.

Cain eyed the two men flanking Mr. Laurence, adjusting his cufflinks as he fought the urge to laugh. "Has it now?"

"It wasn't where you said it'd be. I had to track it down in Rome and nick it from a museum. That's a lot more work than I signed up for. Then, I had to get it here undetected and you know how much I hate this country, yeah?"

"Yes," He glanced around at the graffitied walls and brick path, the old and new blending to create a beautiful ambiance, even if they were in an alley. The Marais district of Paris had always been one of his favorite places, especially in the Fall. It was a shame his associate held such disdain for it. "The English and the French ever at odds. Pity you can't enjoy it."

"Now, about that price,"

"Mr. Laurence," he interrupted. "How long have we done business together?"

"First job was about seven years ago, I think."

"And, in that time, you've risen through the ranks of your group of bandits thanks in no small part to the work I offered you, isn't that right?"

"Well,"

"How much money have you made on my tips? Millions? More?"

He cleared his throat. "Mr. Adamson,"

"That's been our arrangement, yes? I tell you where to find price-less works of art and antiquities, you bring them to me, and I pay you, *well*."

"Yes, but in this case--"

"By 'this case' do you mean that one?" He gestured to the briefcase in Duncan's left hand. The leader of The Mare Boys glanced down at it and back at Cain.

"What do you want it for, anyhow? It's just a rusty old plow blade, so ancient it's got cracks. Thing's fallin' apart."

"Call me sentimental."

"Well, it was a pain in the ass to pilfer, yeah? More work put in, more travel. You owe me--"

"I *what*?!" He took a step toward him, the two men at Duncan's sides swiftly moving forward, their hands now resting on the grips of their guns. "You would do well to remember how you came to your position and who put you there."

The henchman to the right piped in, "You should remember who you're talkin' to, mate."

Cain's eyes flicked to him, a tall, balding, doughy thirty-something with freckles and a non-existent top lip. "You'll be first, then."

"What?"

"Mr. Adamson," Duncan said, calm and condescending. "No need to get worked up. I'm sure we can agree on terms. I just want to be compensated fairly for the extra effort, right? I'm not asking for double. Just another twenty-five percent for Christ's sake. I'm not an unreasonable man."

"I hate to be the bearer of bad news, Mr. Laurence, but unfortu-nately for you, *I am*."

Before he could pull his weapon, Cain had the mouthy henchman on the ground, kicking his leg out from under him and stomping on his dominant hand, crushing the bones. The man cried out in pain as his attacker turned his attention to Duncan's other lackey, shoving the gang leader into him, the two falling to the brick. While they scrambled to get to their feet, he bent over the first man who reached again for his gun, snatching it away, and shooting him between the eyes.

"I don't *like* killing, you know," Cain said, turning the gun on Duncan. "Contrary to popular opinion. I simply refuse to be taken advantage of. Or abandoned. So, this is what we're going to do,"

But, before he could finish his sentence, the second man, a scrawny redhead in a too-big suit sprang toward him. Cain's gun was knocked from his grasp, skidding across the ground and coming to a stop against the dead man's leg. The skinny man punched him in the diaphragm then the jaw. With no air in his lungs, Cain shuffled backward as he hunched over, trying to catch his breath.

"You want to fuck with The Mare Boys?" the man taunted, kicking him in the stomach. "All because you don't want to pay what's due?" He kicked him again, Cain falling to his side, his knees up in the fetal position.

"That's enough, Pats," Duncan warned.

"Nah, nah. He wants to be a big man, right? Comin' at us like he's got the moral high ground or somethin' when we're *all* criminals here. Now, Archie's dead and you say '*enough*'? Sorry, boss, but it'll be enough when this tosser is no longer breathin'." He pointed his weapon at Cain. "I'll give you five seconds to say your prayers and make your peace."

"My prayers," he snorted, sitting up and holding his abdomen. "My prayers have gone unanswered since before the beginning of what you call time. As far as peace, I'm sure I'll never know such a thing, not truly. I have my respites from the pain, of course. Lovers, wine, rare occasions of indulgence in 'controlled substances'. Sleep to dream of something better, a less wretched existence. But, it's hopeless. This is just who I am. Forever."

"I don't know what you're on about but that's enough talkin'." He cocked the gun and pointed it at his face.

Cain rubbed his jaw, his expression smug. "Last words?"

"Make 'em quick."

"I meant," He stood, adjusting his jacket. "Yours."

"I mean it, Pats," Duncan scolded. *That's enough.*"

He laughed, ignoring his boss's warning. "*Mine*? Are you mashed?"

"Sadly, no. Perhaps when I get back to the flat."

"The only place you're going is the afterlife. Say goodbye."

As he began to squeeze the trigger, Cain pounced, gripping the man's wrist and whipping it to the side, the weapon discharging, the bullet whizzing by missing his ear by only an inch. He drove his fist hard into his chest, the force of the punch stopping his heart. He fell to his knees, Cain emptying the clip into the man's head. "I'm afraid I'll never see the afterlife. Not for long enough to remember it, anyway."

"Holy shit," Duncan whispered.

"I'd say that's enough unpleasantness for the day, wouldn't you?" He wiped his prints from the gun and dropped it, again stifling his laughter, the look on Duncan's face the funniest thing he'd seen in quite some time. He'd gone ghostly pale, his eyes like saucers and his mouth hanging open. It was enough to send him into a giggle fit.

Duncan nodded, closing his mouth and opening the briefcase. Cain stepped closer to get a better look at the iron spike inside. The gangster was right; it was rusted and deteriorating. Cracks wrapped around its entirety as if put there purposefully, while the pointed end looked dull. He touched his fingertips to it, a small smile turning up the corners of his lips.

"Time hasn't been kind," he said, taking his hand away. "To either of us."

Duncan closed the case. "I'm torn, ain't I?"

"How's that?"

"On the one hand, it seems I underestimated your temper. On the other hand, I've got two dead mates that need answerin' for."

"Hmm." He bent to pick up the first henchman's gun, looking it over as he stepped closer to the man who, though he tried to hide it, was trembling. "You might be right. Maybe I was a little," He turned his gaze back to Duncan whose Adam's apple bobbed with a hard swallow. "Irrational. I just hate being interrupted. So, now *this* is what we're going to do." He pulled a wad of cash from his breast pocket and handed it to Duncan. "This, the agreed upon price, is for the briefcase. And, this," He took out his wallet, pulled out two Euros, and shoved them into Duncan's pants pocket. "Is for your friends." He yanked the case from his hand. "More than what they're worth, I imagine. I do hope this incident won't affect any future dealings we may have. I rather enjoy doing business with you," He turned to exit the alley, leaving Duncan in stunned silence. "Usually."

Cain left the briefcase in the parlor upon entering his Paris apartment, the smell of boeuf bourguignon filling his nostrils. "Needs more thyme," he called as he locked up. He went to the open living room window and plucked a few leaves from the flower box.

"Thyme or time?" Antoine called back, poking his head around the corner of the kitchen.

Cain held up the herbs and moved to meet him, handing them over and kissing him on the cheek.

"Ah." He bunched the leaves together and chopped them finely, sprinkling them into the pot and stirring the contents. With a clean spoon, he tasted the broth, his eyebrows raising in approval. "You were right, as always, my love." He kissed him back, a quick peck on the lips before pulling two bowls from the cabinet. "So, did you get that antique you've been so desperate to find?"

"I did. It's a little worse for wear than I remember, but that's inevitable, I suppose."

He set the bowls down and looked him over, concern in his eyes as he stared at his boyfriend's face. "You're hurt." He touched his bruised cheek, causing Cain to wince. "Who did this to you? I'll kill him where he stands."

He gently took his hand away and kissed it. "I'm fine. Just an attempted mugging. I got away *with* my wallet, so there's no need for worry."

He cast a skeptical glare as he ladled the stew into the white bowls. "As long as you're all right."

"I am. Now, you sit. I'll finish up in here."

"If you insist." He winked as he walked past, touching his shoulder.

Cain set the table while Antoine sat, bringing the bowls, spoons, and small plates of bread. He poured the wine and lit the candle in the center of the table before sitting himself. "How was your day? Anything exciting in the world of interior design?"

"Exciting, no. Aggravating beyond words, yes." He took a bite, his dark eyes rolling back as he dropped his spoon. "Unbelievable. How do you always know these things?"

"I've had a lot of experience."

"The herbs are," He kissed his fingertips. "They are so good."

"Of course," he teased. "*I* grew them."

"Yes, yes. You used to be a farmer, so you claim. I can't imagine you working in the fields, sun beating down, you getting sweaty, muscles rippling. Huh, I guess I can."

They exchanged flirty glances over the rims of their glasses. Cain took a sip and put his wine down, his eyes never leaving Antoine's face. His thick brows, sculpted nose, and dark stubble covering his chiseled jaw were so sexy, he could hardly keep himself from climbing over the table to get to him. He blinked, clearing his throat and picking up his spoon. "Why aggravating?"

"Well, you know the couple from Troyes who insisted on having the Rue de la Fontaine-au-Roi flat remodeled before moving? The apartment I spent months on with this change or that alteration? The people who cut my budget, then raised it, then cut it again?"

"Yes, I remember."

"Now they've decided they want to move in next week and they insist on it being finished even though the drapes are still on back order because they simply could not live without the gold embellishments and would not hear of an alternative. The *third* kitchen backsplash has yet to be installed because the second must first be removed but the contractor is hesitating because he thinks they'll change their minds *again*, and I'm still waiting on the permit for the fountain they want to install..."

He listened intently, Antoine's run-on sentences and thick accent like a song in his ears. He could listen to him all night, his monologues so full of passion and his expressions so animated, it was like watching a play. As he went on, chestnut waves fell over his sparkling eyes, the hair going unnoticed by him as he continued his ranting. Cain couldn't help but smile, his love for him growing with every word he spoke.

"I'm boring you," he said, tilting his head as if asking a question.

"Never."

"I'm dominating the conversation."

"As long as you let me dominate you later."

He gasped. "How *brazen*." He licked his lips and smiled. "But, I'll allow it."

"What else will you allow?" He asked, tearing off a bit of his baguette.

"Such a flirt."

"And, you're not?"

Antoine laughed. "I suppose we're both guilty of that, eh?"

He flashed a seductive grin. "Among other things."

That night, after chocolate souffle and three rounds of lovemaking, Cain and his lover fell into a deep sleep, Antoine acting as the little spoon as they cuddled in the four-poster bed they shared. While Antoine enjoyed a dreamless slumber, the recurring dream that had plagued Cain for as long as he could remember once again invaded his mind, the memory of the morning his god had abandoned him.

The angel, Gabriel had stood before him, her flaming red hair moving unnaturally in windless conditions, her glowing skin and emerald eyes beautiful and terrifying.

"Please," he'd begged, his knees in the mud, his wife still asleep in the one-room, mud-brick home they shared a few yards away. "I'll do whatever he commands. He can bring my brother back, I know he can. It was a moment of weakness, jealousy. Elohim must know how sorry I am. He must know that I would do anything he asked if he could just bring Abel back to us."

"I am sorry, Son of Adam, but your brother's soul has moved on."

"Moved on to what? What is there apart from this?"

"Another life. Another chance. Right now, his soul resides in the body of an infant born just last evening. It should comfort you to know that there will be redemption for your bloodline, if not for you."

"Does he no longer love me? If Abel is reborn, what was the harm? Was killing him so terrible that it turned the Lord against me forever?"

"It was not what you did to your brother that angered him. It was the lie. You told the Lord your God something that was untrue. He trusted you to be honest with him and you betrayed that trust. There is nothing that hurts him more than that."

"So, he would hurt me in kind?"

"He would use you as an example."

"An example?"

"He hopes your curse will prevent others from making similar mistakes."

"The punishment is too great," he cried, not bothering to wipe away the tears that ran down his ruddied cheeks. "I can not bear it. Forced to wander, immortal and alone. It's too much."

"You will never be alone. Not truly. God will not speak to you directly again, that is true, but he still hears you. He will still listen to your prayers."

"What good are prayers to a deity that refuses to respond?"

The angel knelt, her ethereal face mere inches from his. Her voice lowered as if she were telling him a secret. "Fear not, Son of Adam. Awan is with child."

He glanced back at the house, blinking away more tears before again facing the angel.

"She will, over time, give you seven children. All will remain healthy into adulthood. Show them love, Son of Adam. Nurture your relationships with them and you will never be alone."

Her words echoed in his mind as she disappeared, leaving him sobbing on the ground. He looked over his farm, devastated that he had to leave it. Years of back-breaking labor wasted. That was only a small part of his grief, however. What hurt the most was God's desertion. Cain loved him more than his brother had, more than his parents. He cared for his wife but Elohim was the only one he'd ever truly loved. Without him, he was lost.

Cain woke with a start, thrust from his memories by a too-familiar pain. It started, as it always did, in his legs, like hundreds of tiny, electrified needles sending white-hot jolts through the muscles and skin. *No*, he thought, kissing his lover's shoulder as he slept. *It's too soon.* But, the pain spread, first to his abdomen, then to his chest. He bit his lip to keep from crying out, his features twisted in pain, sweat beading on his forehead. With the first wave of nausea, he rolled out of bed, doing his best to avoid waking his partner. He managed to get dressed without incident, taking his go-bag from the closet before giving Antoine a final glance, a single tear escaping his bloodshot eye. It was time to go.

On his way to the front door, he was hit with another wave of nausea so intense, he had to vomit in the kitchen sink. His head pounded and the room began to spin, his arms going weak as the curse gripped his heart, the searing pain so sharp, he nearly passed out.

He wanted to wake Antoine. He wanted to explain. But, there was no way to, not without sounding like a lunatic. There was no lie believable enough, no story he could concoct that would make sense. The truth, of course, was out of the question. Knowledge of who he really was was reserved for his descendants, not that any of them had ever believed him. He'd have to make an excuse, as he always did in these situations. A vague explanation that would provide an out for him and sew seeds of resentment within his lover's mind. Better for him to be hated than missed.

Choking down the blood coming up in his throat, he took his phone from its charger on the kitchen counter and sent Antoine a text that read: *Had to leave. Business emergency.* Balancing himself on walls and furniture, he shuffled to the parlor, retrieving the briefcase from the closet and making his way to the door. He took one final look at the apartment, knowing it would be at least seven years before he would see it again. "Goodbye for now," he whispered, his voice hoarse. He closed and locked the door, his hands shaking, more from rage than discomfort.

The pain lessened the farther he got from home, disappearing entirely by the time he got out of the city. The train had him in

Montreuil in no time, reminding him yet again of his appreciation for modern advances in transportation.

Old resentments mingled with new as he stared down at his phone, Antoine's face glowing on the screen. It had always been temporary, as was everything in Cain's life. But, he'd had real affection for him, and leaving him hurt more than any curse could. He wanted to make it right. He wanted to one day return, pick up where they left off, bask again in the warmth of his embrace; of his love. He couldn't, he knew. It was far kinder to distance himself permanently, and give Antoine a chance to move on and find happiness with someone new. Someone that he could depend on. He wiped away a tear, swallowed his anger, and put the phone back in his pocket. "I'm sorry, my love."

Chapter 2

F ALLING BACK INTO OLD patterns, Cain did what he always did when his life was abruptly uprooted; he tracked down one of his descendants. Yearning for connection, he traveled to Austria where he found a sixty-two-year-old man named Leon Kussel, one of his son, Lizpha's descendants, living in Salzburg. He realized quickly upon arriving at Leon's residence that there was something sinister about him. As soon as he opened the door his cornflower blue eyes widened as if he'd been startled, but within a few seconds, before Cain could open his mouth to greet him, his features twisted, his pale skin going red, and his nostrils flaring.

"Was willst du?" he asked in German, a language Cain had never bothered to learn but from the way he barked the question, he was already insulted.

"Leon, my name is Cain. Might I come in for a moment? We have much to discuss, assuming you can speak English or French or--"

"Ich spreche zwar Englisch, aber für Leute wie Sie werde ich das nicht tun."

"No? What about," he tried to remember the different languages spoken in the country; languages he knew. "Hungarian? Croatian? My Slovenian is rusty at best but I could muddle through."

"Verschwinde von hier, Araber!"

He didn't know what he was saying, but he was growing more and more hostile by the second. Sweat beaded above his nearly nonexistent lip and he had gone from red to almost purple, his blond, buzzed hair too thin to cover the shine of his scalp.

"Araber?" He'd heard the word before but couldn't place it.

"Ja, du arabisches Stück Scheiße. Verlass mein Haus, sonst bringe ich dich um!"

"Well, this isn't going as I'd hoped. Let me find a translator app." As he reached for the phone in his jacket, Leon reached for something behind the door.

"Stirb, arabischer Abschaum!"

By the time Cain saw the shotgun it was too late. He was on the ground, a hole as big as his head through his chest. The last thing he saw before the world went dark was Leon, his own flesh and blood, though he didn't know it, standing over him, rage in his eyes, spitting in his face.

Cain awoke, like he had thousands of times before, under a sheet in a metal drawer. His hand flew to his chest as he took his first breath in hours, the pain of the gunshot wound faded but not entirely gone. It was always like that, the residual sting of death taking its time in leaving him. Though his flesh was healed, his soul never would be, every death like a tattoo on his heart.

His skin prickled in the cold, steel box, his eyes unable to adjust to the pitch. With little air, there were two ways this could go: either the medical examiner would open the drawer and he'd kill them to make his escape or he'd suffocate waiting, die once more, and wake again. Both scenarios had happened countless times over the years and every time, he was weirdly grateful. At least he didn't have to dig his way out of a grave or swim out of the ocean, drowning repeatedly.

As he settled in for a nap, fighting the shivers that kept him awake, the drawer's door flew open and he was dragged out of it, instinctively grabbing the wrists of his liberator. Within seconds, he was on his feet, struggling with the sheet to keep himself covered.

"Son of Adam," he heard before he saw to whom the voice belonged. The man was perched on an embalming table, his long, thin legs splayed and his appearance ghastly. He wore dusty, black, leather pants with boots to match, a slate-gray henly, and an oilskin duster coat. His skin was ashen, his face gaunt, and his eyes shone in a dreadful shade of gold. Long, black curls hung over his too-broad shoulders while his sharp features and full lips would have made him beautiful...if he didn't look like a reanimated corpse.

"What are you?" Cain asked, his back against the refrigeration unit he'd just been freed from.

"That depends on who you ask." His voice was low, quiet, and had an odd musical quality to it. His accent was one he hadn't heard in thousands of years.

"Angel," he breathed, nearly dropping his sheet.

"Here," He threw a plastic bag in his direction, Cain's clothes and other belongings spilling from it as it hit the yellow tile at his feet. "Get dressed."

He hurried to comply, his mind racing. "I thought your kind no longer spoke to me."

A sickening smirk lifted one corner of his lips. "Call me an exception."

"Why are you here?" he wondered, now clothed, keeping his distance.

"It's frustrating, you know, seeing you die over and over, but never being able to take you to what comes after. It's my duty, you see, to take souls to their next destination. But, your destination is always the same, right back here," He glanced around the room, his nose scrunching in disgust. "To the world my father made for you."

"You're...Death?"

He nodded. "Samael." He looked back at him, his face relaxing. "But, I can't take you, no matter how many times you expire. Your curse makes my job impossible."

"Oh, well, my apologies. I hate to be a source of vexation for one of God's puppets."

His thick, charcoal brows raised. "You mock God?"

"I mock those who serve a god unworthy of their devotion. A god more interested in punishing than loving those he made. He punished my parents with pain and shame. He punished me with banishment." He felt the rage bubbling up in his chest as he put the last of his things in his jacket pockets. "He may be the god of creation but he is *not* a just god. He's more of a monster than I am and believe me, I'm under no delusions. I know what I am."

He tilted his head, his glittering eyes studying Cain's face like a book. He leaned forward causing Cain to swallow his anger and press himself harder against the cool steel. "Fascinating."

"What?"

"You." He hopped down, his boots not making a sound as they hit the floor. He moved closer, towering over him as he continued to stare. The hair on the back of Cain's neck stood on end, goosebumps reappearing on his arms, and bile rising in his throat. "I suppose no bravery is required to speak of the Lord in such a manner when you've already been reprimanded for your defiance...and continue to be." He stepped back, again looking him up and down, arms crossed and expression thoughtful. "We'll speak again, I think."

In a blink, he was gone, Cain left reeling. *What the hell was that about?* he thought. He cleared his throat and his mind, taking his phone from his pocket and checking the time. It was only early evening. He replaced the cell phone and made his way to the door. He was anxious to leave this city, this whole country, even but there was one thing he had to do before he left.

Leon opened the door, greeted by a swift jab to the nose. He stumbled back as Cain pushed his way into the house, slamming the door behind him.

"I remembered where I'd heard that word," the immortal said, taking off his suit jacket and tossing it to a nearby chair. The house was small and dimly lit with only a few ratty furnishings. The walls were mostly bare, the one behind the sofa the exception. It was clad in old Schutzstaffel paraphernalia, a 3'x5' SS flag in the center. It was enough to make him nauseous. "The word on its own is harmless but the way you said it," He hit him again, this time with a right hook to the jaw. He went down, rubbing his face and wiping the blood from his nose with his shirt. "It was clear you meant it as an insult. So, congratulations. You succeeding in offending me." He kicked him in the ribs. "You may share my blood but you are no relation of mine. Consider yourself disowned."

"Was bist du?" Leon said, his eyes wild with fear and his voice a shaky whisper. "Du bist tot."

Not able to understand his questions, Cain ignored them. "Many of my scions have disappointed me over the centuries, mostly because when I explain to them who I am, they think I'm lying...or a lunatic. But, *you*, you represent a failure of everyone that came before. Your father, his father, and his before him." He kicked him again, unwilling to contain his anger. "Your entire line is tainted going back at least a hundred years. There aren't enough words to express how disgusted I am that I spawned such evil and that's coming from *me. Me!*"

"What do you want?" he asked in English, his accent heavy and eyes filling with tears.

Cain knelt next to him, eyes ablaze as he noticed the man's Gothic cross necklace. He snatched it from his neck, breaking the chain. "I wanted a family. I wanted us to be friends. But, that's impossible now, as you've made abundantly clear, and seeing what you are has changed my desires. Now, all I want from you is death."

He tried to sit up, tried to escape, but Cain used his empty hand to slam Leon's head to the floor. Dazed, he winced in pain, covering his head with trembling hands.

He held the pendent close to his face, showing it to him as if he'd never seen it before. "The man you claim to worship would be sorely disappointed in you." He grabbed his face, forcing his mouth open as he tried to fight back. With pressed lips and flushed cheeks, he poured the jewelry, pendant first into Leon's mouth before holding it closed. He kept his hand over his nose and mouth making it impossible for him to breathe. He grabbed his wrist in a feeble attempt to free himself but Cain was determined. He leaned in close and through gritted teeth, his voice little more than a growl, he spat, "Choke."

Chapter 3

H E COULDN'T GET OUT of Austria fast enough and soon found him-self on a plane to New York. He hadn't been to the city since the early nineties when he'd discovered his youngest daughter living there, surrounded by dozens of her ghoulish creations. He won-dered if she still called it home and if she did, if she was happy in her depraved existence. He hoped she was for as much of a monster as she'd become, he still held a soft spot for her, though he didn't like admitting it to himself. He'd kept an eye on her, from a distance, secretly peeking in on her life from time to time. She'd built armies, businesses, and untold amounts of loyal followers. She was a queen to her people and there was a part of him that couldn't help but be proud. A lump of guilt formed in his throat as he thought about her, his favorite child who was destroyed by his selfishness and his wife's insecurity, the only person left on Earth who truly knew him. He thought about the night she died, a memory he'd replayed in his mind thousands of times if not more. She'd known Lilith was dangerous to their family but he hadn't cared, too lonely to put them first.

Cain had felt the urge to leave his home in Ur. He'd gathered what little belongings he could into one cart and his grandchildren in another. "Can we go to Eridu?" his daughter had requested. "I'd like my child to be born there, at home."

He'd agreed and set the course. As he began walking, Lilith at his side humming to herself, he'd listened in on Allydia and her husband's conversation. They'd been as quiet as they could be but he had excellent hearing. Even with a cart separating them, he could make out clearly what was being said.

Farhan had begged her not to go, saying she was too close to delivering and she should be resting. But, she'd been determined to stay with him. "I can't abandon my father," she'd told him.

"He has a wife to look after him," he'd rebuffed. "Please, my darling. Think of your family."

"He is my family. He has never abandoned me, so I will never abandon him. He needs me."

"He has Lilith. I know you do not approve of her but she treats him with kindness. She will take care of him as you take care of me."

"Lilith is a poison, a black stain on his heart. He will see that eventually and when he does, he will need us to comfort and keep him. Do not worry, husband. I will be fine."

Now, sitting in the stuffy plane, he wished he could take it back. He should have left them that day, his daughter and her children. They would have been better off. Looking back, abandonment would have been kinder than what transpired only a few hours after they'd left Ur. He hadn't wanted to be without his family and that was selfish. It would have been better to simply break her heart.

The plane landed in France for a layover and upon departing, Cain was gripped yet again by the sudden need to flee. He hadn't even made it out of the airport so while doing his best to hold himself together, he booked another flight, the one soonest to depart. It was a one-way flight to Edinburgh that was already boarding. He hurried onto the plane and sat in a window seat, the pain searing through him as he tried to hide it, coughing blood into a handkerchief and discretely tucking it back in his pocket. Panicked stares from the other passengers let him know he wasn't hiding his affliction well at all and if he didn't want to be thrown off the plane, he'd have to come up with a satisfying lie.

"Cancer," he said to an older woman across the aisle who looked particularly frightened. "Nothing contagious."

He saw the relief in her face then the guilt. "I'm so sorry, sweetie," she said, reaching into her purse and pulling out a cough drop. She held it out to him and he politely took it, useless as it was.

"Thank you." He sat back in his seat and closed his eyes, holding tight to his arms to keep from shaking. Soon, they were in the air and once they were over the ocean, his symptoms subsided. Two hours had passed by the time he woke to realize he'd fallen asleep as had the woman across the aisle. It was a smooth flight, with not much turbulence to speak of. Perfect for getting a nap in.

"Amazing, isn't it?" Samael said, from the seat next to him.

He jumped, looking around to see if any of the other passengers had seen him appear from thin air. They hadn't seemed to.

"The ingenuity of humans. The creativity. They never cease to amaze me. That bit of God in them that allows for innovation, for imagination. Someone really looked to the sky, saw a bird flying, and thought, 'I could do that,' and they made it happen. The artistry. It is truly inspiring."

"What are doing here, angel?" he asked, his nerves getting the better of him.

"I was bored."

"Bored?"

"Yes. A flight attendant perished just there," he pointed to the back of the cabin where a curtain separated it from the kitchen. "Not five minutes ago. Now, my job is finished and I am again left to my thoughts, and believe me when I tell you, my thoughts are grim."

"How can your job be done? Shouldn't you be ferrying the girl to one place or another?"

"I already did, hence my boredom."

"That was quick."

"Time works differently for me."

"I see."

"I'm curious, how does one such as yourself live?"

Confused by the question but afraid not to answer, Cain told him, "Forever, it would seem."

"Yes, but humans are pack animals, dependent on the company of others. Yet, you have no pack, no tribe. How do you survive? It must be a terribly lonely way to exist."

"It is."

"Is that why you seek out those of your lineage? For a sense of belonging?"

He dropped his chin, hardly able to admit it to himself let alone the angel of death. "It's all I want."

"Then why not start again? Find a woman, procreate. Bring your new family along on your travels."

"My travels?" he said, annoyance now coloring his voice. "You say that like I go on vacations."

"A lot of people live that way, moving from place to place. Military families, celebrities. Why not you?"

He shook his head, sure the angel could never understand. "It's not the same. For them, ordinary people, life is short. They have children and grandchildren and they die without ever knowing what will become of the people that came from them. But, I never die, not permanently. So, when my first son, Enoch passed on, I swore to never let myself feel the pain of that loss again. I kept track of my descendants, of course, but I will not create more. Still, I long for connection. I've contacted those of my line but the conversations never go as they should. They never love me. They never accept me."

Samael's sparkling eyes fell to his hands crossed in his lap, his features pinched as if in sadness.

Cain chuckled at the sight. "Are you feeling sorry for me, angel?"

He lifted his gaze to the seat in front of him, his head tilted in thought. "Perhaps I am. Strange," He looked at him, brows furrowed and face sullen. "The world's first murderer has a heart."

He laughed again, amused by the angel's realization. "I am only human, after all."

"Indeed." And with that, he was gone, disappearing with no reaction from the other passengers. Had he been invisible to them or were they just so caught up in their own distractions they hadn't noticed? Or, perhaps he'd imagined him there, a distraction of his mind to keep him from wallowing in his grief, his ex-lover occupying his thoughts.

Cain shook the conversation from his mind, taking his phone from his pocket. He'd had it on do-not-disturb since leaving Paris, unable to bring himself to check for messages from Antoine. It had been days since he'd left so he knew there would be many. With a deep breath, he opened his texts, deciding that hearing his voice via voicemail was still too painful.

Where are you? the first message read. *Are you serious?* read the next. Dozens of texts filled the screen. *Why are doing this? How could you do this to me? Is there someone else?* On and on they went, his heartbreak evident. He hated doing it, hated leaving with no explanation. But, what explanation could he give him? He could never tell him the truth and no lie would make sense. It was better to stay gone, a clean break. Besides, it had been less than a year since they'd met. Antoine would move on in no time and Cain would, too recover. Maybe he'd take another lover or a few. It's what he needed. More distractions. More ways to pass the time that would never truly end.

Chapter 4

U PON ARRIVING, HE CALLED movers to collect his things from Antoine's flat. He scheduled them for a time he knew the apartment would be empty, instructing them to use the key he'd kept in a flower pot for emergencies. They'd be in and out in no time, Cain only keeping a closet of clothing and a few pieces of art in the home he'd shared with his former lover. It was the smart thing to do, he'd decided, never keeping too many belongings in one place. At any moment, he could be forced to abandon them, along with the people he invited into his life.

"Iona," Cain said as he entered the antique shop, one of many businesses he'd acquired over the years. It was a perfect place to sell, and hoard, all of the trinkets and bobbles he'd collected throughout the centuries.

The shop girl smiled politely from behind the counter. "Mr. Adamson. Haven't seen you in a while. How have you been?"

"No worse for the wear. How's business?"

"As good as ever, sir."

"Excellent. You should expect a shipment from Paris in a few days. Don't open it, it's just some of my personal things. Clothing and the like. I'll be in to fetch them as soon as I can."

"Of course, sir," she said, tucking her black hair behind her ear. "Can I get you a cup of tea? I have a pot on in the break room."

"That would be lovely, thank you."

As she disappeared through a door at the back of the shop, a man in an expensive-looking suit approached him, a fake smile plastered on his face. He was selling something, no doubt about it.

"Giovanni La Rosa," he greeted, staring into his eyes and holding his manicured hand out for Cain to shake, which he did.

"Cain Adamson."

"May I ask, are you the proprietor of this establishment?"

"I am."

"It's a beautiful store." He glanced around then again made too-direct eye contact. "Must keep you busy."

"Not especially. The girl and her manager run things well enough without me having to do much but sign checks."

He offered a forced laugh, smacking Cain on the shoulder. "To be your own boss. It's the life, is it not?"

"I suppose."

"I'm having a get-together tomorrow night. You should come." He dug a card out of his jacket pocket and held it out.

He took it and looked it over, nothing but an address in white on a black background. "A...get-together?"

"Very exclusive. VIP's only." He eyed the break room door, Iona still nowhere to be seen. "Beautiful ladies. Models. Molto bello."

"Ah. I think I understand."

"Wonderful," he said, clapping once, the sleazy smile returning to his lips. "I'll see you at midnight, eh?"

"Perhaps." He tapped the card to his fingers. "It could be just the thing I need."

"Eccellente! I'll see you then." He slapped him on the back with a little too much force and exited the shop.

"Hello, can I he--" Iona said, rushing from the back room, stopping mid-sentence when she saw no customers. "Oh. I thought I heard the bell."

"Just someone leaving. Don't worry. They were selling, not buying."

She looked puzzled but didn't ask what he meant. "Your tea's ready." She brought it to him, a tiny spoon still in it for stirring. "Sorry it took so long. I had to wash the cup."

"Don't give it a second thought." He took a sip. "Brodies?"

"Yes, sir."

"Very good, thank you."

She nodded, looking pleased with herself and taking her place behind the counter. While he drank, he wandered the shop, looking over the items he'd accumulated and discarded, some he'd forgotten he had like the Remington 1 typewriter he'd purchased in the summer of 1874. He'd spent hours on end typing up poems and short stories. Nothing that would sell, of course. Just tales he made up to entertain himself. Now, it sat on a shelf amid first editions of Dickens, Poe, and Shakespeare. A relic of times long gone by, just like him. Maybe he would go to La Rosa's "party". Drowning in a sea of women and alcohol was as good a way as any to numb the pain of losing the man he loved. Besides, what else did he have to do?

The next night, Cain spent three hours at Giovanni La Rosa's extravagant apartment drinking Barolo, making small talk with degenerate men he had more in common with than he liked to admit, and drowning his sorrows in the body of an auburn-haired temptress. Her skin was soft and fair, her eyes chartreuse with full, jet-black lashes, and her lips were painted an unnatural shade of red. She smelled of lilies and chardonnay and no matter how beautiful or enthusiastic she seemed, he couldn't think about anything but his ex. It was *his* eyes he wanted to be looking into. *His* body underneath him. *His* cries of passion. The woman was lovely enough, she just wasn't Antoine.

He got back to his flat, drunk and half-asleep, stumbling in the dark to find the lamp next to the sofa. His fingers fumbling, he finally clicked it on, jumping back at the sight of his former lover sitting there, arms folded, and face flushed with anger.

"Antoine?" He stepped back, not trusting his eyes. He rubbed them, hoping to clear the alcohol's blur to no avail. "Is that you?"

"Of course it's me, who else?" He snapped in his thick, French accent.

"H-how did you find me?" He took another step back, bracing himself against the wall in an effort to keep from toppling over.

"Oh, please, like you're so mysterious? You're an antique dealer, not a government spook."

His brows furrowed as he stared and wished he was a little more sober.

"Fine!" He stood, moving to meet him across the room. "I tracked your phone. Are you happy? You've driven me to stalking."

"But, why..." His voice drifted as did his mind. He was getting dizzy. If he didn't sit soon, he would pass out.

"You sent movers. *Movers!* That's when I knew you would never return. That you were done with me for good. So? What was it, then, mm? I disappointed you somehow? Angered you? Bored you?"

"You did nothing."

"Then, what? What drove you away? We were happy, I thought."

"We were. You, you, my love, are perfect. It's me that's wrong."

"Wrong?"

"In so many ways."

He stepped closer, his nostrils flaring as he sniffed Cain's neck. "*A woman?* Is that it? You grew tired of me and went back to your old ways?"

"No. I could never grow tired of you. Believe me." He tried to touch his cheek but Antoine slapped his hand away.

"But, you turn your affections to her, this cheap perfume-wearing harlot?"

"H-how did you know she was--"

His voice raised as he begged to understand. "How could you do this to me? After everything I've given you? My love. My devotion. Why did you throw me away like so much trash? Why was I not enough?"

"I can not explain. There's no way to describe," He stopped, his brain foggy as it searched for the right words. "It wouldn't make sense to you. You wouldn't believe me. No one ever believes me."

"There are three things I believe. First, that I deserve better than to be treated as you've treated me. Second, that you have no remorse for what you've done to me, and, third,"

Cain's eyes filled with tears as he listened, the haze of drunkenness threatening to overtake him at any moment. He was so lost in the sadness of his beloved's face, he didn't see him reach into his jacket pocket. Didn't notice him moving closer. He didn't see the knife.

"I believe that if you will not have me in this life, I will meet you in the next."

A sharp pain spread through his lower abdomen like fire up to his chest. He looked down to see Antoine's blood-soaked hand holding the hilt, slicing upward, then pulling out. "No," he grunted, holding his wound. His back hit the wall as he stumbled, slipping down to a seated position, his hands shaking more in fear than in pain. "Please. You don't understand. You don't know what will happen!"

"You will die, is what will happen. I will toss some things around, empty your wallet to make it look like a burglary. No one will ever know I was here. And, when my day comes, I will meet you in another life, one where we can start again, unburdened by whatever it is you think I won't understand."

"No," He shook his head, the color draining from his face. "Please, my love. If I die, *you* will die."

He knelt in front of him, brushing the hair out of his eyes before kissing him on the cheek one last time. "I died the day you left me."

Chapter 5

B Y THE TIME CAIN woke up, Antoine was dead, curled in a heap on the floor in the entry. He crawled to him, his chest caved in with grief. He rolled him to see his face, now pale and slack-jawed, his eyes still slightly open. "No," he whispered, tears like waterfalls down his cheeks as he gathered his lover in his arms. He held his head close to his chest and sobbed into his hair, kissing him gently at the temple. For hours, he sat like that, morning stubble growing on his face as the sun rose, its pink and orange glow through the living room windows breaking his heart further. The world had moved on from the night's cruel circumstances but he never would.

"I am sorry, Son of Adam," he heard from behind. It was Samael, lurking in the shadows, no doubt there to fetch Antoine's soul and take it to God knows where.

He didn't turn, instead holding tighter to his lover's body. "He couldn't have known. He didn't mean to," He stopped with the crack in his voice, wiping away a tear before finishing his thought. "He never would have done it if he'd known it would have been him that would perish."

"I know that."

"So, he will not be punished too harshly? He'll be spared the torments of Hell?"

"Rest assured," Samael said, placing a thin hand on his shoulder. "Human souls don't go to Hell. That's a punishment reserved for beings more...knowledgeable."

"I'll try not to be insulted since that does come as a relief."

"Why would you be insulted?"

He sighed, resting the corpse's head gently on the floor and standing to face the angel, all fear of him seeming to disappear in his bereavement. "Never mind. What are doing here, angel? Have you come to take him to the next life? I can't imagine he's headed for Heaven after committing murder."

"He now resides in the isolation of Purgatory where he will reflect. In time, he will be born again as someone new, as all souls are." He looked him over, one thick brow raised. "Well, nearly all."

"This," he said, pinching the bridge of his nose before letting his hand drop limply at his side.

"This, what?"

"You asked me why I don't find someone, build a life. This is why. Death follows me. Wherever I go, it finds me. It nips at my heels like a dog begging for food and I feed it. I toss it my scraps when I don't fill its bowl outright. That is what you're really here for, isn't it, angel? To pick at the carcasses left in my wake? Like a vulture circling, you bide your time, hungry for the next meal I serve up to you?"

"You look like your mother, you know? And, a little like your father, too," he said, seeming to ignore his harsh words. "Though your temperament is less," He paused, biting his lip as if in thought. "Whiny."

"My father was...*whiny?*"

"Yes, well, your anger is justified whereas he was just ungrateful. Like a child. Though, I suppose he was, in a way, a child. The first of your kind, God's great experiment. Creatures of the Earth endowed with what you call souls. He was new to the world, to life, as a child is. It is no wonder he could not handle the responsibilities bestowed upon him. More guidance was needed, it would seem."

"My father was a fine man," he said, only half believing it.

"That depends on your standards, I guess. He was kind to you, until your exile, but he barely acknowledged your sisters. When you and Abel were gone, he gave all of his attention to your brother,

Seth, fearful that he might lose yet another son at any moment. He pleaded for your return, as did your mother. They never stopped wishing for you to come home. Now, they wait, still, pacing the halls of Paradise with your siblings, to this day begging my father to forgive you."

"You," He swallowed the lump in his throat, his lip beginning to quiver. "You've seen them? They don't," He brushed away another tear, trying desperately to hold himself together. "They don't hate me?"

"Of course not," the angel said, so matter-of-factly, Cain couldn't tell if he was joking or not. "They forgave your evil deeds long ago. It will take more than time, though, for things to be set right in my father's eyes."

"Nothing I can do about that, is there?"

"Nothing *you* can do, no."

"Wonderful."

"I am sad for you, Son of Adam. You should not have to toil on this planet, unloved and resentful. Your curse should come to an end."

"A kind sentiment but your words are hollow. The Angel of Death can't undo what God himself has set in motion."

"Not alone, I can't."

His ears perked and his brow lifted. "Speak plainly, angel."

"My father's slumber approaches. If Heaven's Gate is destroyed while he rests, it will not be repaired for over two centuries. The link will be broken. His power will not be able to reach you. You will no longer be under his command. The immortality, the compulsion to flee, the harm inflicted upon you transferring to those who inflict it, will all be gone. Your curse will be broken."

His throat went dry, his heart racing. "But, I-- I don't understand."

"By the time repairs have been made, you'll be long dead, either in Limbo or on to another life."

"The curse," He swallowed hard, glimmers of hope filling the darkness in his mind. "Broken?"

"It will not be easy, of course. You'll need help. An army, for starters. Not to mention--"

"Whatever it takes," he blurted. "I'll do anything you ask. But, why would you help me? It can't just be because you feel sorry for me."

He stared, the look in his eye sending shivers down Cain's spine. He crossed his arms and dipped his head a little before answering, "I have my reasons."

In a flash, he was gone, leaving Cain alone and confused. He knelt next to Antoine's body, covering his mouth as he again began to cry. He was overwhelmed by so many conflicting emotions. He would take the day to mourn, to show his beloved the respect he deserved. Then, he would consider what Samael had told him, and decide if he could be trusted.

That night, as the city slept, Cain dumped his lover's body in the North Sea, his heart breaking as he watched it sink. Back at his flat, he cleaned blood from the floor and burned his suit, the dry clean only fabric ruined by stains of his blood and Antoine's. When all evidence of the night before was cleared, he began to relax, his thoughts shifting to Samael and his offer.

Before he could trust him, he needed to do some research. He looked online for mentions of the angel in religious texts, discovering that he was known to sympathize with humans, condone sins, and was considered evil by many religions. In some texts, he was affiliated with Lucifer, in others it was *he* who tempted his mother in The Garden, deemed the commander of the snake that led to humanity's Fall. Had he been there to gift his parents with knowledge or to curse them? Did he truly care for humans or did he simply hate God?

"It doesn't matter," he muttered to himself. Either way, he was on Cain's side. He would help him to end his wretched hex and he would finally be free.

Chapter 6

C AIN SPENT THE DAY making calls, instructing his Realtor to sell off hundreds of real estate holdings. Over the years, he'd collected houses, condos, and apartments all over the world, renting them out when he was inevitably forced to leave them. They brought in a substantial income but not nearly the amount he would need to pay for a private military outfit. He'd keep a few dozen places for himself, one in every major city he liked to frequent and a few in more remote locations, places he could retreat to when he needed a break from humanity.

As the sun set on another day without Antoine, a regretfully sober Cain nursed a headache with too much ibuprofen, not realizing that what he needed was food. He'd forgotten about it, eating, the way he had the last time he'd been this depressed; the night his daughter was turned into a monster.

A knock came on the door just as his head stopped pounding. Someone from the shop downstairs, no doubt, needing help with an invoice or an irate customer. It was the one drawback of spending time in this particular flat. Any other time, Iona or her manager, Angus, would figure things out on their own. At worst, they'd send an email. But, when he was close by, they came to him directly for any number of minor issues from a power outage to a lost shipment. "Children," he whispered, getting up from the couch and shuffling to the door.

"Can I help you?" he asked the man as he opened it, knowing his tone was sharp but not caring in the slightest.

The man's sapphire eyes widened, staring at him, his expression a strange combination of adoration and resentment. After a few seconds, he cleared his throat, flashing a flirtatious grin and pushing past him into the apartment. "I'm told it is you who needs help."

He closed the door, turning to watch the man wandering curiously around the room, looking at the art on the walls, and running a finger over the curtains. "You're one of them?" he guessed, noticing the same lack of manners and respect for boundaries Samael had displayed when he'd been there. "An angel?"

"I used to be. One of Daddy's favorites, actually," He ran a delicate hand over the arm of the sofa, strands of straight, blond hair falling over brows so pale, they could hardly be seen. "Until I wasn't."

His throat became a desert as the angel locked eyes with him, panic and hope mingling in his stomach as he fought the urge to run. "I can relate to that," he said as calmly as he could, determined not to let the angel sense his apprehension. "What did you do to incur his wrath?"

"I stood up for myself." He sat on the couch, stood, sat, and stood again. "Bouncy."

He was stunned. "You refused to submit to God's commands?"

"No," He moved closer, taking his hand and giving it a squeeze. "Your father's."

His eyes saucered, rage replacing all other emotions as he realized who he was talking to. "*Lilith*."

"Hello, husband."

He lunged forward, pushing her against the wall, his hand tight around her neck.

"Hey, careful! You'll give me a bruise."

He seethed, eyes wild and teeth bared, his voice little more than a growl. "I should kill you where you stand."

"*Kill me?* For what? Giving you exactly what you wanted?"

"What I wanted was for my daughter to *live*, not be made into the fowl creature you turned her in to. I had to marry my granddaughters off to the first men who would have them to protect them from her. From *you*." He punched her, the man's face she was wearing removing any guilt he might feel for striking a woman. She was in a man's body, after all.

"Watch the face!" she protested. "I'm trying to be pretty, here."

He punched her again, this time splitting the man's lip.

"Will you stop that?! You know I can't defend myself."

"You could," he baited, taking a step back and spreading his arms. "Go ahead. Hurt me. *Kill me*. I beg you."

"Very nice," She rubbed her throat then put her hands on her hips. "I come all the way from Hell to help you break your curse, put on this ridiculous body to please you, and you thank me with violence and death threats. Typical."

He looked her over, taking note of the dark wash jeans and black tee shirt she wore, the sneakers, and the silver chain bracelet. Thin and muscular, he was attractive but not overwhelmingly so. A little young for his taste, probably in his early twenties. "I don't under-stand. Why should this body please me?"

"I was told that your tastes have...evolved."

"My *tastes* have remained as they always have,"

She arched an eyebrow and tilted her head as he continued.

"Varied."

"Yes, well, I'm considering dumping this and slipping into someone a little more comfortable. Men's bodies are so weak, their most vul-nerable bits on the outside, hanging like fruit waiting to be plucked. Feels like a design flaw."

"Get out, witch!" he barked, throwing a finger toward the door, a vein throbbing in his neck.

"Or what?" She smiled, closing the space between them and glid-ing her fingers up his arms to his chest. "You'll smack me around some more? I'll tell you a secret...it doesn't hurt me."

"I don't need you," he said through gritted teeth. "I can do this on my own."

"You can not. Raising an army takes more than money. You need men to be devoted to you or, at least, to your cause. Tell me, husband, how much experience do you have manipulating men? Because, between you and me, it's kind of my specialty." She pressed her lips to his but was quickly pushed back.

"Fine. I'll go, give you a day or two to accept what you already know to be true."

As she slinked to the door, he called after her, "What's that?"

She smiled again, her hand on the doorknob, her eyes on him. "That you *do* need me, and, you always have."

In the quiet of the night, Cain sat on the roof overlooking the deserted street below. He'd spent hours there in dark solitude, his mind swirling. Should he accept her offer to help or attempt to murder her? He'd fantasized about it a million times, killing her, wrapping his fingers around her throat until she breathed no longer, watching the light in her eyes dim, and the color drain from her face. But, there was no way to kill an angel, as far as he knew and that's what she was, even if only technically. "Fucking Lilith," he muttered, shaking his head and resting it in his hands. "Is this what it's come to, Grandfather," he prayed, unsure if God was listening or if he was just talking to himself. "Am I to rely on the witch that ruined my life even more than you did to save me from my torment? I would rather die a thousand more times than be near that creature again but," He squeezed his arms to keep from shaking. "Lord, I can take this wandering no longer. The loneliness, the death. It is too cruel. If there's a chance for me to be free of it, I must take it." He sighed, looking up at the stars and breathing in the early autumn air. "Even if it means collaborating with the one I hate most in this world. Once again, Grandfather, I ask your forgiveness, though I don't expect to get it.

Chapter 7

T HE NEXT MORNING, CAIN was woken by pounding on his front door. Wrapping himself in a paisley, silk robe, he wondered if the building was on fire or if Iona was just concerned about the return policy…again. Annoyance turned to confusion when he opened the door to find the sex worker he'd been with a few nights before. He'd forgotten her name, if he'd ever bothered to learn it at all, so he was unsure of how to greet her. Still groggy from too little sleep, he said the first thing that came to his mind. "How do you know where I live?"

"Sam told me," she said, giving him a wink and pushing her way inside.

"Sa--," He closed the door, the realization striking him. "*You*."

"Do you like it?" Lilith said, gesturing to the body she now occupied. "I mean, I know you do, that's why I chose it but," She cracked her neck, wincing in disgust. "It's old."

"That woman is no more than thirty."

"It has aches. *And*, its stomach hurts. I had to heal six different ailments just to make it tolerable."

"Dramatic as ever, I see. What do you want?"

"More time but that's not in the cards." She traced the edge of his robe's belt with a rose gold painted fingernail. "You've held up well, husband."

He batted her hand away.

She smiled as if amused and walked around him to the sofa where she sat, crossing her legs and adjusting her skirt to cover her knees. "Playing hard to get? That's fine. You'll relent, eventually."

"Why are you here, witch?"

"So rude. I'll disregard your attitude for now, seeing as how we have much work to do and very little time."

"Little time? Doesn't Elohim sleep for more than two hundred years?"

"My father is not the problem. It is my siblings that concern me. Apparently, Daddy dearest saw our little plan coming and sent a few of his favorites to spoil our fun. They already take steps to prevent us from succeeding."

"More angels?" He sighed, rolling his eyes. "Anyone you can't handle?"

"Most are harmless. Raphael, Uriel. I've never tangled with Barachiel but I hear he's more of a danger to himself than anyone else, at the moment. There's Gabriel. She could be a problem. They aren't the real threat, though."

He lifted a brow, hands folded in front of him as he stood over her. "No?"

"When my brother liberated me from my prison, others followed."

His eyes widened, a shiver running up his spine.

She smirked, sitting back and twirling her hair. "I see I don't need to remind you of what happens when demons escape Hell."

"No," he said, chewing on his lip. "You do not."

Thousands of years ago, he couldn't remember exactly how many, Cain had been, for the dozenth or so time, following someone he believed to be Lucifer. He'd tracked him to Akrotiri, a city long forgotten on what's now the island of Santorini. It was beautiful, he remembered, with comfortable homes and brightly colored frescoes, paved roads lined with shops offering everything from fruit to clothing, and stunning views of the Aegean Sea. It had been one of his favorite places to visit until that dark and hellish night when he'd been so desperate for peace, desperate for death, that he walked in on something that would haunt him for the rest of his agonizingly long life.

Lucifer, in the body of a tall, blond man, had been hunting an escaped demon and after two weeks of searching, he'd finally caught up to him in an alley during a light rainstorm. The demon, sickly pale and drooling black fluid, begged to stay, even getting on his knees and pleading with his jailer to be let go. "Please, Watch Keeper. I can take no more suffering! I beg you, let me go!"

But, Lucifer just clicked his tongue, giving his head a quick shake, his eyes, like a predator's, fixed on his prey. "You know I can not." He placed his hand on top of the demon's head, whispering something Cain couldn't make out. After a few seconds of twitching and screaming, a black mass appeared to peel away from the man the demon had been possessing. It slithered down to the ground, disappearing in the shadows. When it was done, Lucifer crouched to check the man for signs of life. He found none, Cain surmised, by the bereft sigh he heard escape his lips.

Cain remained hidden as Lucifer left the alley, following him for several minutes until they came upon a two-story house overlooking the water. It was painted in vivid blues and yellows with bronze embellishments on the roof and windowsills, and the home was surrounded by flowering gardenia shrubs. He watched from afar as Lucifer entered the building, unaware that he was being tailed.

Outside, Cain paced, practicing what he'd say, how he'd beseech him, beg him to end his misery by killing him once and for all. If anyone could, it would be him, he'd thought. He was nervous then, though he'd spoken to him many times before. He'd tried to befriend him out of sheer loneliness, every attempt shot down by a dismissive and uncaring Guard of Hell. But, now he was desperate, miserable. He wanted it, *all of it,* to end and Lucifer's wrath was his only chance at getting what he needed.

After thirty minutes of building up his courage, he walked up to the house and knocked on the door. No answer. He knocked again, three loud raps, and waited. He knew he was still inside, he'd been watching. He'd never left, he was simply ignoring him. Irritation overriding his fear, he opened the door and let himself in.

No lamps were lit on the first floor, the clay bowls of olive oil sitting with untouched wicks on tables and window ledges. Moving quietly to the staircase, he could see a dim light through a cracked door at the top. Had Lucifer already gone to bed, exhausted from tracking and exorcising the demon? If he woke him, he'd be angry. *Good*, he'd thought. When wanting someone to kill you, it helps if you piss them off.

He crept up the steps, peeking his head into the room just enough that he could see Lucifer was not asleep...or alone.

"Again," Lucifer ordered, lying on his back and grabbing the linen covered behind of a woman perched on top of him. She obeyed, slapping him across the face, causing his lip to bleed. He laughed, smacking her backside. She bent down to kiss him, his hands running up her back. "How do I taste?"

"Divine," she said, sending them both into fits of laughter.

That voice, he'd thought, recognizing it even after a thousand years. "Ibnat?"

"Father?" Allydia yelped, turning and covering herself, her expression as horrified as he knew his must have been.

Lucifer laughed harder, sitting up and grasping her by the scruff of her neck. "Son of Adam! What an unwelcome but amusing surprise. I must say, as annoying as you are, you did make one gorgeous and, dare I say, adventurous daughter."

She slammed her hand into his chest, knocking him on his back as he continued to chuckle. "It is not what you think, Father."

"Of course, it is!" Lucifer chortled. "Why do you lie? The man has eyes. How much did you see, Son of Adam? Me putting it to her or just the last few moments as we geared up for round two?"

"Close your mouth!" she shouted.

"A departure from what you said less than an hour ago but as you wish."

"He means nothing, Father."

Lucifer put his hands behind his head and clicked his tongue. "If I had feelings, I think they'd be hurt."

"Father," But he was already gone, backed away and flying down the stairs.

Racing away and taking refuge in the alley where a corpse seemed better company than his own daughter, he doubled over, hands on his stomach, heaving until he threw up his dinner. How could she allow herself to be defiled by such a creature as Lucifer? Had she learned nothing from his time with Lilith? He was just as brutal as she was, a monster.

He'd always known that Allydia drank blood to survive, as was her curse, but seeing it with his own eyes and in such depravity turned his stomach. Obviously, Lucifer had corrupted her even further. There would be no redemption for her, as he was sure there would be none for himself.

"I thought I'd have more time before my brother caught on but I should have known better than to underestimate him," Lilith said, tearing him from his memories. "Smart as a whip, that one."

He shook the revolting images from his mind. "Get out."

"Excuse me?"

"If Lucifer's on Earth, he'll be coming for you as well as those demons and when he does, I don't want to be anywhere near you."

She tilted her head like a confused puppy. "Are you afraid of him? He wouldn't hurt you. He values his comfort."

"I said get out!"

She bolted up, studying his face, an amused grin perking up her lips as she realized. "Oh, you do not fear him. You're still upset that he fucked your daughter."

He slapped her, a twinge of guilt like a light peeking through his endless rage.

"A firm hand," she mocked. "It is as if we are still married."

"I never struck you when I called you 'wife'."

"Only because you were afraid to. Seems your instincts were better then."

"You think you frighten me? *You*?"

She shrugged.

"Do your worst." He held out his arms, once again inviting her to inflict pain that she would soon feel herself.

She cracked her neck, her demeanor going cold. "All right." With a flick of her wrist, the television sparked, the screen cracking. The lamps and overhead light also shattered along with every cup and dish in the apartment. Anything that could be broken was broken, bits of glass and porcelain littering the floor.

"Now you're just being childish."

"Hmm?" She waved her hand, invisible claws ripping through canvases of priceless art that hung on the wall behind him.

"That was the original Portrait of Dr. Paul Gachet!"

"I don't know what that means."

"Van Gogh! I paid eighty-three million dollars for that in the nineties! Do you have any idea how much it's worth now?"

She flashed a condescending glare. "Whatever you could fetch for the frame, I'm guessing."

"How did you know about Lucifer and my daughter, anyway?" he blurted, too irritated to stop himself.

"Sam caught me up. Do you yield?"

"Do I, what? To you? No, I do not. You need to get as far away from me as you can because I will not--"

She snapped her fingers, exploding the kitchen cabinets and bedroom door, bits of wood flying in all directions. "I can do this all day, you know."

He sighed. "I know."

"Come now, husband. Let us not fight. You don't really want me to hurt you, do you?"

"More than anything."

"Stop it." She smiled, inching closer. "We both know that's not true. Well," She reached for his robe's belt, swiftly untying it and slipping her hands inside. "Not *entirely* true."

He pushed her away, covering himself. "Stay away from me, witch!"

"Oh, come on! I haven't felt the touch of a man in five thousand years. Besides, we are still technically married. Perform your husbandly duties. It's cruel not to."

"I owe you nothing, you vile bitch. After everything you've done, you're lucky I'm willing to let you walk out of here with your head still attached."

"And force me to find a new body?" She scoffed. "You wouldn't do that." She closed the space between them, gliding her hands over his hips and standing on her toes to reach his lips. "You like this one too much."

He grabbed her by the throat and swung her around, slamming her into the wall so hard, the plaster cracked. Noses inches apart, he squeezed until he heard her sounds of struggle. Cutting off her oxygen wouldn't kill her, of course, but it was enough to remind her of who he was. "You are a contemptuous, wicked, disgusting abomination. Malevolent doesn't begin to describe your villainy. My hate for you runs deeper than the sea and if God himself commanded it, I wouldn't give you a second of pleasure. All I wish for you is suffering."

"Lies," she choked. "You want me. I can feel it."

"You've gone mad. Even madder than you used to be. Hell must have done a number on you if you believe I still desire you." He let go of her throat and spoke directly in her ear. "I wouldn't touch you with a stranger's dick."

She touched his cheek and licked her lips. "Then why is yours harder than Roman concrete?"

He stepped back, just noticing his body betraying him.

She moved closer, again untying his robe. "I realize we have our issues, like any couple. But, you have to admit, when we were together, alone, in the dark, desert breeze on our exposed skin, bodies entwined," She threw off his robe and pulled him close. "We were a force of fucking nature."

She kissed his neck, getting out of her clothes and pressing herself to him, wrapping one leg around him like an invitation. He tried to fight it, tried not to give in. *She's a monster*, he told himself. But, soon, despite his better judgment and common sense, he relented, throwing her over his shoulder and carrying her to the bedroom.

He tossed her onto the bed, grimacing at her flirtatious grin. With a growl in his throat, he climbed on top of her and plunged inside, his fingers again wrapped around her neck because even if he couldn't control himself, he would make damn sure she knew he could control her.

Chapter 8

A FTER HOURS OF NEAR rabid copulation, Cain and Lilith fell unconscious on stained sheets, the bed frame barely surviving the event. Memories like dreams played in his mind, visions he'd had a million times before.

"He could not help you if he wanted to," the angel, Gabriel had told him when he'd finished vomiting in the Akrotiri alley. He'd jumped, not realizing she was there until she spoke. Perhaps she hadn't been.

"Have you come to mock me?" he'd asked, wiping the bile from his lip with the back of his hand.

"No. I have come only to tell you what I have in the past. You will not die until God demands it."

"And, when will that be, hmm? A year? A thousand? Ten?"

"I am not privy to that information, yet."

Her melodic speech and unnatural movements had always given him a sense of unease causing him to show more respect than he thought she deserved but in that moment, he was too angry to watch his tone. "And, Lucifer with my daughter? Is that another one of God's punishments?"

Her luminous face scrunched, a sign of irritation that he chose to ignore. "That has nothing to do with you, I assure you. My brother is," She looked in the direction of Allydia's house then back at him. "Impulsive. If it makes you feel any better, he means her no harm."

"It does not. Had he taken her by force, I would have only him to blame. I would take a blade to his throat, or worse."

"That would not kill him."

"But, it would hurt him as he has hurt me. It would quench my thirst for revenge. It would be what he deserved. That is if he had been the sole perpetrator. But, it was the two of them, both equal in their wickedness. The fornication alone is bad enough but when I saw her drink of his blood…" He covered his mouth, his stomach threatening to spill its contents once again.

The angel looked annoyed, like there was something she wished to say but refused to. He'd imagined she'd wanted to lecture him on being a better father, to tell him to accept his daughter for who and what she was. But, he could not. It was too grotesque. Too corrupt. He would rather grieve her as human than accept her as the monster she'd become.

She levitated off the ground, rising to his height to make eye contact so intense, he had to take a step back. "I will tell you once more and never again, Lucifer can not end your life. Nor I, nor any of my siblings save one and Wrath will not do so until Elohim himself commands it." She floated closer, the heat radiating from her making him sweat. Her voice changed, lowering at least two octaves as she stared him down, her words biting. "Accept your fate, Son of Adam."

He woke with a start, Gabriel's words repeating in his mind like a warning. His eyes drifted down to see his arm around Lilith's shoulders and her head on his chest. It was enough to make him sick. He hated her, and himself. He wanted to hurt her, to kill her. He wanted to sneak away and run from her. He wanted to slap himself in the face for being so easily seduced. But, mostly, he wanted to die.

Why would she help him do it? It didn't make sense. Lilith never did anything unselfishly. What, exactly, was in it for her?

He bolted up, pulling on a pair of black, silk sleep pants. "Get up, witch," he barked, kicking the side of the bed.

Her eyes fluttered open as she performed a sexy kitty stretch, her breasts peeking out from under the sheet. "Husband," she said with a yawn.

"Why are you here, really?"

She looked up at him with feigned innocence. "I can't aid you in your time of need out of the kindness of my heart?"

"We both know you have no heart. Only lust, petty jealousies, and hunger for power. So, what did Samael promise you?"

She sat up and sighed, running her fingers through her hair. "That is none of your concern. Just trust that our objectives align."

"Trust? *You*?"

She inspected her nails as she spoke, her dismissive demeanor fueling his rage even more. "I fail to see any other option."

"What is it, Lilith? Men? Freedom? What could the angel of death have offered you that would convince you to help me?"

The corner of her mouth lifted in a small smirk as she finally looked him in the eye.

"Oh," he said, his arms crossing over his chest. "It's Earth, isn't it?"

Her smile broadened. "Not the *whole* Earth."

"He promised you an Earthly kingdom, didn't he? That moron! Is he unaware of the atrocities you perpetrated when last you took power for yourself? The lives lost?"

"As if you care about such things."

"You had entire countries subjugated. You think I don't know what you and my daughter were up to after I left? Why do you think I stayed away?"

"Honestly? I thought you were having a temper tantrum and that one day, you'd be back, ready to reign along with us."

"A tantrum? I stayed away because you disgusted me. You still do."

She looked down at her naked body and then back up at him. "Strange. You did not seem disgusted when you had your tongue in my--"

"Enough!"

"Worry not, husband. I'll carve out a corner for you. I hear America's nice, full of sex, hatred, and pretty items for purchase. All of your favorite things. It will be yours to rule as you see fit. Unless," She got to her knees and ran her fingers over his bare chest. "You'd like to reign at my side. You know how I hate being lonesome."

He pushed her to her back, walking to the end of the bed as she sat herself up. "I have no appetite for power. I've seen what it does to lesser men. I've seen what it did to you. You deserve power less than the false god who made you."

Her face twisted in offense. "My father is a lot of things but a false god is not one of them. Being cross with him, even justifiably, does not change who and what he is. Believe me, I've hated him a lot longer than you."

He scoffed, shaking his head.

"Have you forgotten what he did to me? Forcing me to be a helper to your father who saw me more as a servant than a teacher? Banishing me not only from Eden but from Heaven as well when I refused to bow to Adam's whims? Turning my siblings against me when I turned to magic to reclaim my power? My own father *hating me* for daring to have a thought of my own? You think you're lonely here in this paradise he handed to you, never able to settle, and losing your family; your choice, let us not forget." She walked on her knees to meet him, eyes piercing and cheeks reddened. "Let me tell you something, you small, human man. You don't know alone. The abyss God leaves when he abandons. It is a vacancy that nothing can fill. The pain sears like a hot poker and it never lets up. You can still pray. He won't always answer but he always hears, his time of rest aside. Your soul is forever tied to him but my thread has been cut and the torment of his absence is worse than anything your puny human mind can comprehend so do not think for a moment that you have a monopoly on hating God. Still, no matter how cruel, he is and will always be, undeniably, the Almighty, most high, creator of all, your God. Doing this, destroying the gate, is worse than defiance. It's declaring war on God. It would be a mistake to underestimate him. So, yes, Samael promised me the world if we succeed. It's the only thing worth the risk. Because, if we do this and fail, the only safe place to hide will be the cage I just crawled out of."

Chapter 9

C AIN TOOK LILITH TO Louden's for a late breakfast, too hungry and too anxious to continue arguing. She had been right, he knew. He'd seen firsthand the destruction God could inflict when pushed. But, what would the consequences be for him, really? There was nothing he could imagine being worse than what he'd endured over the last six thousand years.

"It is a bit industrial, is it not?" Lilith said, glancing around the restaurant.

"Stop complaining," he told her. "Eat your food."

"It's brown."

"Banoffee pancakes are almost exclusively comprised of sugar, a food you've yet to try but one I think you'll appreciate."

"Because you know me so well?"

"If memory serves." He lifted his cup and took a sip of tea.

She took a bite, her brows raising as she chewed and swallowed. "Not bad. Not my preferred breakfast but,"

He glared at her over his cup.

"I know, I know," she said, rolling her eyes. "Not in your presence. Wouldn't want to upset your delicate sensibilities. As in the past, I will refrain from eating my food of choice when we are together."

He grunted in disgust at the thought of what she considered food. "Thank you."

"Anything for you, husband. As always."

"Just finish your pancakes."

They ate in silence for a while, Cain catching himself looking too long at her left shoulder, the strap of her sundress falling ever so slightly off of it, her skin prickling in the cool autumn air. She didn't feel the cold, though. She'd always been indifferent to temperature, somehow never sweating or shivering. Even as she was occupying a human host, no level of heat or cold seemed to affect her. After years of being with her, fooling himself into believing she was truly his wife, it was that lack of feeling that had reminded him that she was not of this world.

"Cain?" a woman's voice called from across the room.

He looked over to see who it had come from, his stomach dropping when he found her. "Shit."

"It is you!" The woman stood, approaching their table with determined steps, her cheeks flushing.

"You know this woman?" Lilith asked, the jealousy twinging her voice causing his heart rate to increase.

"I used to. Come on." He threw some money on the table and grabbed her by the arm, hurrying her out of the building.

"Another lover? You have been busy, haven't you, darling?"

"It was years ago and we only dated for a couple of months."

"Dated? Well, it seems my suspicions are justified."

"Suspicions?"

"That there are others in your heart leaving no room for me."

"Hey!" the woman yelled, following them down Fountainbridge.

He held tight to Lilith as he ordered under his breath, *"Keep walking."*

The woman ran up, yanking on his jacket sleeve and spinning him around, forcing him to let go of Lilith's arm. "You owe me an explanation," Stick-straight strands of dark hair stuck in her rosy lipgloss as blue eyes narrowed. "Don't you think?"

His own eyes pleaded with her as he warned, "It's in your best interest to flee."

"Cain, darling," Lilith inserted. "Aren't you going to introduce me to your," She looked her over, clearly not impressed. "Scraps?"

"*Excuse me?!*" the woman huffed.

"Lilith, please," he hissed. "We're in public."

"What?" She giggled. "I'm as harmless as a kitten."

The woman folded her arms, her vengeful gaze falling back on her ex. "You can't just ghost people. It's rude. I deserve a real explanation."

"It is as I told you."

"Told me? A text saying, 'I must move on' isn't an explanation, it's an affirmation. So, what? You dumped me for this skank?"

Lilith leaned in to whisper in Cain's ear, "What is a skank? I feel insulted but am unsure of why."

"Deirdra, my sincerest apologies. I should have gone about things differently. I see that now. You have every right to be upset with me but rest easy knowing that I have suffered horribly in the years since our tryst and you are lucky to be free of me. Now, if you'll excuse us, we really should be going." He reached for Lilith's hand but before he could take it, Deirdra slapped him hard across the face.

Before he could blink, Lilith was on top of her, slamming her down, and cracking the sidewalk with her back. She flew into a rage, punching her repeatedly as he tried to pull her away.

He scolded her like an untrained puppy. "Lilith, no. I said no." But, she continued, breaking the woman's wrist with her mind. Deirdra cried out so Lilith swelled her tongue. Soon, she couldn't breathe let alone scream.

"Lilith, stop this now!"

She whipped her head around to speak to him directly. "She struck you. Her disrespect will not go unpunished." She flicked her wrist, snapping the woman's neck.

"For fuck's sake." He snatched her up and dragged her away, doing his best to hide his face from the crowd of people gathering to witness the brutal event.

"She got what she deserved," Lilith said, calm returning to her voice.

He rushed them back toward his flat, sighing in agitation. "This may come across as mean-spirited but would you kindly shut the fuck up?"

Back at the apartment, Cain took his go-bag from the closet and stuffed his laptop into it. "We have to go."

"Already? I was just beginning to like it here."

"You caused a scene. Police will be looking for us."

"So?"

"We can hardly win a war against the Almighty from a cell, as you well know."

"Or, and I'm just thinking out loud but, why could we not just kill any authorities that give us trouble?"

"I suppose we could if you're content with being hunted by every cop in Europe whilst hiding from Lucifer *and* putting a private army together. Am I forgetting anything or is that our complete agenda for the foreseeable future?"

"Oh, there is plenty more."

He sighed. "Wonderful. It's settled then. We're going. Hopefully, we can get out of town without being seen and quickly enough that if questioned, we can say we weren't here."

"But, where will we go?"

"I have a place in London."

"Where is that?"

"South of here. We can take the train and be there by tonight."

"Whatever you think is best. Cain, darling?"

He took her arm and escorted her out of the apartment. "Yes?"

"What is a train?"

Lilith watched from her seat as they passed fields and forests at unimaginable speed. "Incredible."

Cain locked the door to their cabin and sat across from her, his muscles finally relaxing. "I don't think anyone recognized us."

"Of course, they didn't. You're paranoid."

"Maybe, but when you've been alive as long as I have, you learn that it's better to be safe than sorry."

She smacked her lips in response.

"It's a very common saying for a reason."

"If you say so."

"You shouldn't have killed that woman."

She peeled her eyes away from the window to cast him a confused glare. "She harmed you. I could not let it stand."

"Why not?"

She dipped her chin, her eyes softening. "You know why."

"I do," he said, closing his eyes and shaking his head. "God help me, but I do."

"Don't be troubled, husband. We got away, did we not?"

"For now, but there are eyes everywhere. Cameras in every pocket, on every building. The world is not as you remember it."

"But, you are." She slipped off her shoes and used a toe to fondle the hem of his pants.

"Lilith,"

"What? The door's locked." She stood from her seat and hopped in his lap, lifting her skirt. "And, I'm wearing nothing under this dress."

"Lilith, this can not continue."

"Come on," She unbuckled his belt and whipped it off before freeing his most delicate parts of their cotton prison. Leaning in and licking his earlobe she whispered, "Play with me."

He tried to stop himself, tried to think about anything else. But, the blood had left his brain for destinations south, and without realizing it, he'd slid his hands underneath her dress and used them to grip her backside. After a few seconds of teasing, she placed him inside, a small gasp leaving his lips as they were pressed to hers. "This...can't...keep...happening." But, as he buried his face in her neck, he knew he was lying to himself. He hated her with every cell in his body. More than God. More than anything. But, as true as that was, it was also true that he wanted her just as much.

Chapter 10

T HE NEXT MORNING, CAIN awoke in his London flat to a phone call from his Realtor. Offers on his properties were already rolling in, mostly from asset and investment management companies. He told him to accept all cash offers that were at or above asking and to email him the paperwork. He ended the call, got out of bed, and quickly showered, desperate to get Lilith's scent off of him. "Idiot," he called himself, scrubbing lipstick from his chest. "How could you be so stupid?" He leaned against the shower wall, his forehead resting on his forearm as scalding water rained down his neck and back, unable to tell who he was more angry at, her or himself. She was digging her hooks in, he could feel it. Five thousand years and mountains of hate between them and she could still put him on his knees with the snap of her fingers, figuratively *and* literally. "Fucking moron."

Freshly clothed but still unshaven, he entered the living room to find his nemesis on his laptop, the click-clack of her fingernails on the keyboard driving him mad within seconds. He observed her for a few moments, allowing his disdain to fester, knowing it was his only protection from the witch and his own stupidity. "What are you doing?" he finally asked, standing in front of her, anxious to get out of town as quickly as possible.

"I've discovered the internet," she said, her eyes not leaving the screen. "You can do anything now. Reach anyone. Reach *everyone*."

"Yes, I know how the internet works." He closed the laptop as she yanked her hands away and rested them in her lap.

"I can work so much more efficiently. All I need is a well-placed mouthpiece to throw the masses into disarray. Someone they already trust. Have you heard the term, 'shock jock'?"

He ignored her, leaning on the table and looking down at her. "We need to talk about Lucifer."

"He is far from here, do not worry."

"How can you be sure?"

She reached for her black, leather purse, slid it across the table toward her, and pulled out her phone, flipping it around to show him the screen. "I get updates from the decoy."

He squinted to see the text messages but she shoved the device back in the bag before he could make any words out. "Decoy?"

"The demon keeping my brother occupied. They're currently in a place called New Jersey."

"Well, that's a bit of good news, I guess."

"Did you know there are shops now that carry magic supplies in exchange for money *in the open?*"

"I did know that, yes."

"We *have* to go. I need many things."

"Go alone. I need to arrange for my Paris flat to be cleaned."

"Could we not do that ourselves? I've seen pictures of Paris on the internet. It looks beautiful. I would love to see it."

His eyes fell as he shook his head. "I just left there. I can not return for--"

"Seven years. I remember. Father's cruelty knows no limits. I'm so sorry, husband."

He leaned closer, fury burning in his chest. "Stop calling me that. Our union was broken long ago."

"Is that what you tell yourself? Still?" She sat back, her eyes twinkling with amusement. "Even after last night? And, the night before that? And, this morning?"

The muscles in his jaw twitched as he gritted his teeth.

"Come on, you don't want me venturing out alone. What if I get impatient? I would hate to cause another scene. You should stay close, don't you agree? In case I need reining in?"

"Fine," he growled. "But, only because we're on a clock. The faster we gather what's needed to destroy Heaven's Gate, the sooner I'll be free of you."

She softly chuckled as she twirled her hair. "Darling, you will never be free of me."

Sage and lavender perfumed the air in the Broadway Market shop. Shelves lining all four walls were filled with jars, crystals, and books, tarot cards, jewelry, and herbs of every sort imaginable. Cain watched like a babysitter as Lilith happily plucked items from their places, holding them to her chest like precious gems. She was a kid in a candy store and if he didn't despise her so much, he might have found her giddiness endearing. Perhaps he did, despite himself.

Her smile faded as he paid for her sack of ingredients and upon leaving the store, she let out a frustrated sigh. "There were a few good herbs but most of those things were utterly useless. I suspect what I need will only be found where I left it."

"And, where's that?" he asked, his shoulders slumping.

"It is..." She stopped in her tracks, her face scrunching as she stared through the window of a coffee shop. "Who is that man?"

He followed her gaze to a man in his late twenties, give or take, with Middle Eastern features wearing a black suit Cain guessed cost only about one hundred pounds at H&M and a sloppily knotted blue tie. "I've never seen him."

"Are you sure? He feels so...familiar."

He squinted, noticing the five o'clock shadow and serious expression. Looking him over, his eyes fell to his waist where he saw a holstered gun. "He's either a cop or a criminal, by the looks of him. Either way, we should steer clear."

"Yes," she said, eyes still glued to the stranger. "Keep a low profile. I understand." As the man took a sip from his cup, Lilith whispered, "Alshier min alraas." He choked on his coffee, his free hand flying to the back of his head. He looked behind him and to both sides but saw no one. In a blink, a lock of chestnut hair appeared in Lilith's hand.

"What are you doing?" Cain asked, his accusatory tone seeming to please her.

She looked up at him with innocent eyes. "Nothing. Just curious."

"Mm, hmm."

"Are you jealous?"

"That would please you, wouldn't it?"

"Yes." She flashed a wide grin as they began walking. "Do not worry, my love. It has always only been you in my heart, no matter who shared my bed after you left me."

"So, where is this trinket you need?" he asked, desperate to change the subject.

"My last home on Earth before my brother so brutally wrenched me from it. Be a dear and charter a jet. It's far."

"My phone is dead," he lied. "Give me yours."

She handed it over without hesitation, her attention now on the scenery of the park across the street. While she was distracted, he put a tracker app on her phone before making his call. He'd never been able to trust her. There was no reason he should start now.

Chapter 11

SEVEN HOURS AND ONE intolerably awkward flight later, Cain and Lilith stood at the base of a massive staircase outside the ruins of a long abandoned temple in what used to be called Ur.

"I forgot how cool it gets here at night," he said, buttoning his suit jacket.

"When was the last time you were here?" she asked, sadness and nostalgia drooping her eyes as she stared at the once magnificent building.

"I'm not sure. A hundred years, at least. Probably more."

"So, you saw its deterioration?"

"Not exactly."

She glared up at him. "What do mean?"

"I've only ever seen this place in this state. I avoided it when I heard you had taken up residence here. It was thousands of years before I felt comfortable coming back."

She smacked her lips in annoyance and looked again at the ruins, breathing in slowly as if to savor the air around her former home. "They worshiped us, Allydia and I. You should have seen it. The adoration. The fear. It was glorious."

"Fear, I can believe but adoration? Somehow I doubt it."

She cast a sideways glance at him. "Excuse me?"

"It's much more likely they behaved as they thought you'd like in an effort to avoid being tortured, or worse."

"They loved us. We were gods to them."

He scoffed. "Tell me, witch, do you love *your* god? Or are you just afraid of him?"

She crossed her arms, her lips forming a pout as she thought about how to answer the question.

"I'm right, aren't I?"

"You should stop talking now."

He laughed, following her into the shell of the old temple. Sand and dust tickled his throat and burned his eyes as he watched her feel along the walls, their cell phones' flashlights the only illumination in the ancient room. "What are you looking for?"

"A compartment," she told him. "I hid things there when last I was here. Things too powerful for even my right hand to see."

"My daughter was *not* your right hand. She was your captive."

She spun to face him. "She was not! I will have you know, we were the best of friends. We ruled *together*, as you and I will when this is over."

"I told you, I have no interest in ruling anything, let alone at your side."

"Fine," She went back to her search. "Perhaps your daughter, *my friend*, will feel differently."

He marched toward her, gripped her arm, and lowered his head to look her directly in the eye, his voice dropping an octave and his tone deathly serious. "You stay away from my daughter, do you hear me, witch?"

"Like you care." She yanked her arm away and pushed past him. "I asked Samael if you had reconciled and he confirmed what I suspected to be true, that you continue to punish her with your absence, as my father punishes me."

"I do not punish her."

"What do you call it, then, when a father abandons his child and threatens to kill her if he ever sees her again?"

He clenched his jaw.

"Oh, yes, he told me about that, as well. You saw her on some battlefield somewhere centuries ago and threatened her life because you, what? Saw her eat some people? Seriously, I don't understand what the big deal is. So, she's a vampire. So what? You're an immortal serial killer. You're basically the same thing."

"She's not herself. She's not even human. She is only what you made her, a blood-thirsty monster with no soul."

"Forgive my candor, husband but are you stupid?"

"I must be. I'm here with you."

"She did not lose her soul just because I changed her physiology. You would know that if you hadn't fled in the night without giving me a chance to explain fully."

"I have seen what she is capable of. You've been away. You don't know the extent of her cruelty even to her own kind."

"Forgive me again but I am fairly certain that's a trait she inherited from you, not me. Here," She pressed against a crumbling wall, a stone sliding back to reveal a hidden compartment. She reached her hand in and pulled out a small mortar and pestle. "Found it."

"That's it?" he asked, turning his light to the dark granite grindstone. "Seems like we could have gotten one of those anywhere."

"Not like this. It's enchanted."

"Of course, it is."

"I spelled it with my own power so that no matter who uses it, the spell will work. This, along with a few ingredients, will make our army unstoppable."

"I see." He took it from her, shoving it in his breast pocket. "At what cost?"

"Nothing is free in magic, as you well know. But, fear not. I would never put you in harm's way."

"Uh-huh."

"I knew you would return here, eventually," a scratchy voice said from the entrance of the room.

"Corson?" she said, flashing her light in his direction.

"Yes," he said, stepping closer.

"What are you doing here? You were instructed to watch over the others until I returned."

He sneered as two more men came in behind him, their clothes in tatters and their noses dripping with black fluid.

"What is this?" she snapped.

"Judging by their body language," Cain said, unable to hide his amusement. "I'd venture to guess it's a mutiny."

"Is that true, Corson? You would dare defy me?"

"I would dare hold my fate in my own hands rather than hope someone else will give me what I desire."

"And, what is it that you desire that you fear I will not grant you?"

He pushed Cain down, knocking his phone from his hand as his head hit the floor, then snatched Lilith's phone and threw it at her feet, grabbing her wrist and asserting, "Freedom."

She cocked her head, Corson and the others flying in different directions, their backs crashing into the decaying walls as she grumbled, "Fucking demons." She picked up her cell and shut off its light, looking down at Cain and ordering, "Stay behind me."

What happened next was a blur of partial light and kicked-up sand, Cain doing his best to avoid the confrontation. In the dark, he heard screams of pain, thuds of bodies hitting walls and the ground, and the snapping of bones. He heard Lilith reciting spells in Arabic and Aramaic and felt an unnatural wind blow through the room as demons barked at her to stop.

"Hide, husband!" he heard her call. Shining his light in her voice's direction, he saw her being dragged out by two demons, the third rushing toward him. He pulled his arm back, gearing up for a punch but the demon moved too quickly. He felt his hands on both sides of his head and then, with no time to defend himself, the crack of his spine as his vision went from blurry to nonexistent.

Cain woke early the next morning, the sun barely risen, its rosy light filtering in through the entrance and cracks in the walls and ceiling. He sat himself up, finding his phone in the rubble and dropping it into his breast pocket where he felt the mortar and pestle still in place.

"You must find her," Samael said, his ominous presence giving Cain chills.

"Must I?"

The angel shrugged. "That is up to you. However, should you wish to be free of God's curse--"

"Why did you send her? To torture me further?"

He dropped his chin, a puzzled expression covering his blanched face. "Are you not happy to see her?"

He stood, brushing the dust from his jacket and slacks. "Why on earth would I be happy to see her?"

"She knows you, who you are. What you are. What you are forced to endure. She clings to your side, defends you. You complain about being alone yet you would leave the one who loves you to die at the hands of demons?"

"She *is* a demon and she knows not of love, only obsession."

"What else *is* love to humans but connection, obsession, and familiarity?"

"She turned my Allydia into a monster. I will never forgive her."

"She did that for you, to please you. To keep you."

"She's insane."

"Yes, I believe she is. That does not change the fact that if you have any hope of severing God's tether to this world and to you, you will need to work with her. You need her, her...skills."

"Perhaps, I do but it's a skosh irresponsible, promising her a kingdom, isn't it? Knowing what she did last time she held power on Earth?"

"Probably, but it was the only way. Regardless, she is the key to your freedom. Save her, save yourself. Do not and continue to suffer. It is at your discretion."

He disappeared, the tension Cain hadn't realized he was holding releasing. He breathed an annoyed sigh, cracking his neck and exiting the building. "Goddamn angels."

Chapter 12

BEFORE HEADING TO THE airport, Cain decided to stop by Eridu, the first city he built, named for his eldest son, now fallen to ruin. Bile rose in his throat as his chest caved with sorrow at the sight of it in this abandoned condition. He was the first to abandon it, of course. He'd had no choice. But, his best and worst memories were all made there: his wife, Awan, doting on him, birthing all of his children, and eventually succumbing to disease. It had devastated him to leave and more so to take his children with him, especially Allydia. He could still hear her pleas, sobbing over her mother's grave, begging him not to make her leave it, the only connection she had to her. He had so many regrets when it came to his children, especially her, the biggest one being having brought Lilith into their lives. Had he not done so, not been so lonely and desperate for companionship, not been so selfish, maybe his sons wouldn't have left him. And, Allydia would have died that night in her birthing tent, a pain that would have crushed him but that he could have endured. Instead, he'd made a deal with the witch that stripped her of her humanity, her sweet nature, and by his actions, her children. He would never forgive himself for his part in what happened to her and he would never forgive Lilith. The demons could kill her for all he cared. It's not like she didn't have it coming.

Cain settled in his seat, eager to get back to London and away from the country he once called home. The plane was crowded and smelled of vomit but anything was better than staying there for another moment. Demon attack aside, the desert sands held too many memories, the good ones more heartbreaking than the bad.

He checked the tracker app he'd put on Lilith's phone. It had her over the Mediterranean, on a plane, he presumed. Either on her way to meet him in England or being held captive, he didn't care. If she survived her scuffle with the demons, he hoped she'd stay away. She wouldn't, he knew but a man could dream.

Seething in his seat, he went over it again and again, Samael's words of warning. He'd made it clear: if he refused her help, he was doomed to fail. The last few days with her, the run-in with the demons, and the depressing trip down memory lane would all have been for nothing. He would wallow in his melancholy for a time, distract himself with sex and alcohol, and live with yet another regret. Samael was right. Without Lilith's help, his curse would remain and he couldn't bear the thought of it.

He closed his eyes for a nap, hoping for a respite from thoughts of the witch. Instead, his dreams were lousy with her, images of her nude form writhing underneath and on top of him, flashes of her defending him to his former lover, and her voice as she protected him from the demons saying, *Stay behind me*. He jerked awake as the plane made its descent, her voice still ringing in his mind. He rubbed the sleep from his eyes and took a sip of water, confused and disgusted with himself. He wanted to blame her, tell himself that she was forcing him to dream of her. That it was one of her powers. But, it wasn't and he knew it. It was him. She was in his mind because, on some level, he wanted her to be. He leaned back, letting out a frustrated sigh and muttering under his breath, "Idiot."

Back in London, a woman he'd never met paced in front of his door. Long, dark curls bounced down her back as she moved, her folded arms covered in a black and white striped sweater, her eyes somehow familiar. "Can I help you?" he asked, inserting his key in the lock and opening the door.

"Cain Adamson?" she said in a thick, French accent.

"Yes."

"I am Elise, Antoine's sister. I need to speak to you."

He held his face still, though the mention of his lost love's name threatened to bring tears to his eyes. "Come in."

She followed him inside, closing the door behind her but staying close to it. "I'm hoping you can help me locate my brother. He hasn't checked in and that's not like him. I moved to the States some years ago so since we can't see each other that often, we text every day. That is, until recently."

His stomach turned, his mind racing with memories of Antoine's face as he stabbed him, finding his body, and dumping it in the sea. "That would be my fault, I'm afraid. We broke up, you see, and I handled things poorly. He deserved more than a dismissive text. He's probably off on vacation somewhere, cursing my name and sipping daiquiris on a beach out of range. I'm sure he'll turn up in a few days."

She bit the inside of her cheek, her expression changing from worried to suspicious. "So, you haven't seen him?"

"I'm afraid not. Not since I left Paris."

"That's interesting because he texted me that he was waiting for you in your flat in Edinburgh and if you didn't turn up there, this was the next place he'd look." She theatrically glanced around the room. "I don't see him here. Are you telling me he hasn't been by?"

"He hasn't but if he contacts me, I'll be sure to tell him you're looking for him." Hadn't he said no one had known he was in Edinburgh? Was she in on his plot to kill him? He reached past her to open the door, praying that she'd leave with no arguments.

She smacked his hand away, her eyes bulging with contempt. "But, you *were* in Edinburgh when he was there."

"I haven't been to Scotland in years but I do keep a flat there. It's understandable that he might--"

"Lies! I went to your antique shop there and the girl told me you'd just left." She stepped closer, accusations and rage flaring in her irises. "What did you do to my brother, Mr. Adamson?"

He did his best to appear innocent while giving her a vague but honest response. "No harm came to him by my hand, I swear it."

"Why don't I believe you?"

He took a breath, offering more honesty despite her attitude. "Because I am a deceitful man and you're not an imbecile but I am not lying about this. I would never hurt Antoine. I loved him deeply."

"Loved," she said backing into the door and fumbling for the knob. "Past tense?"

"I had to leave him. I had no choice but I did love him, for a while. I still do, it just," He could see the fear in her eyes, the shakiness of her hands. "Can not be."

"Why not?" she asked, her voice trembling.

He didn't know what to say. There was no explanation he could give, not without telling her who he was and what happened to her brother. She'd never believe him. She would assume he was a madman, a murderer. She already did, he could tell. She wasn't wrong but he didn't kill Antoine. Not really. There would be no convincing her of that, though.

"It was nice meeting you, Mr. Adamson." She scrambled to get the door open and slipped out, never taking her eyes off him. She closed the door and through the wood, he could hear her speedy footsteps racing down the stairs.

He grunted in irritation, sick to death of traveling and starving. But, he couldn't stay there now, not with Elise getting close to the truth. His stomach growled and he ignored it, deciding to pick up lunch on the way back to the airport. "Time to go...again."

Chapter 13

H E MUNCHED ON A chicken, bacon, and avocado baguette as he followed the dot representing Lilith on his phone's screen. Sitting in the airport surrounded by people, his blood pressure began to rise. What if Elise brought her suspicions to the authorities before he could get out of town? And, where could he go to make sure he wouldn't be discovered? Europe was out, at least the UK. He couldn't step foot in France for a while. Eastern Europe was stressful and he stood out like a sore thumb in Asian countries so hiding out in one of them was out of the question. He blended in just fine in the Middle East but being there, immersed in the countries and cultures he'd help create, his home, was too gut-wrenching. The twenty-four hours he'd just spent there was more than enough for a while.

He finished his food and looked again at the screen. Lilith's dot had stopped moving. She was in New York. Or, at least, her phone was. He groaned, the idea of being that close to New Jersey, that close to Lucifer, making him question even more if he should find his devious ex, save her, or leave her to die at the hands of her own kind. He didn't want to have a run-in with Lucifer, of all people and if he found her before Cain could, she was already gone, back to the cage he'd put her in five thousand years before. "Screw it," he whispered, getting up and heading to a terminal to buy a ticket. She could be in need of rescuing and, as much as it killed him, he needed her to end his curse. He would find her in New York and together they would end his wandering once and for all.

The plane landed at JFK at four EST leaving plenty of time for him to track Lilith down before getting some much-needed sleep. Eager to get it over with, he exited the plane as quickly as he could but was halted at the gate by four armed police officers.

"Cain Adamson?" one of them said, approaching him with cuffs in hand.

"What's this about?" he asked, knowing the answer already but feigning ignorance in the hope that it would help convince them of his innocence.

"We'd like you to come with us, sir. We have some questions regarding an Antoine Moreau."

"Antoine? What has he done?"

The men looked at each other, unconvinced glares between them letting him know they didn't believe his performance.

"Come with us, Mr. Adamson," the first cop said, stepping closer.

"What for? I have nothing to do with whatever shenanigans he's gotten mixed up in. We haven't spoken since I ended things."

"That about a week ago, right?"

"Give or take, yes."

"Mm, hmm."

"If he's done something illegal, I assure you, it has nothing to do with me. Now, if you'll excuse me..." He tried to walk past them but the policeman with the attitude was having none of his nonsense. He took him by the arm, spun him around, and slapped the cuffs on.

"Have it your way. You're under arrest for the murder of Antoine Moreau. Anything you say can and will be--"

"This is outrageous!" Cain fumed. "When my lawyer hears about this--"

"Yeah, yeah. Save it for the judge." They walked him out of the airport, embarrassment flushing his cheeks and anxiety flipping his stomach. He couldn't find Lilith from a cell and being locked up in jail meant he'd be a sitting duck for the demons that took her, should they be done with her and wished to torture him for sport. He'd have to find a way out of this and fast.

Thrown in a cell and told to sit down and shut up, Cain stood in defiance, arms crossed and back against the wall, facing the door as to stare angrily at anyone wearing a badge that came into view. He had one cellmate, a scruffy man of about sixty wearing a raggedy blue baseball cap and stained tee shirt. "What are you in for?" the man asked, shoulders hunched and elbows on his knees as he sat on the cot next to him.

"They think I killed someone. I didn't...technically."

He looked up at him with steel blue eyes. "Technically?"

"The truth is, *he* killed *me* which means that he unwittingly killed *himself*." Too irritated and anxiety-ridden to keep his mouth shut, he kept talking, the stench of cheap booze coming off the prisoner all but guaranteeing he wouldn't remember this conversation, anyway. "There was no way for him to know what would happen. I never told him, of the curse but I didn't kill him. That's not to say I don't belong in a place like this. The things I've done would turn your hair white,"

He paused, glancing at the man's head. "Whiter. But, regardless of what I do or do not deserve, I can't stay here and I definitely can't go to prison. In twenty or so years, when I haven't aged or worse, if they give me the death penalty and I wake up in a prison morgue without a trace of the poison they'd injected me with in my system, I'd be found out, studied. Experimented on like a rat in a cage. They'd think I was a medical marvel, some kind of genetic freak or alien from another planet."

"You going for an insanity defense, then?"

He smiled to himself, his eyes falling to the floor. "I suppose I could. The truth does tend to get me written off as a maniac."

"Adamson!" a guard called, shuffling along the narrow hallway and stopping in front of the cell. "Let's go."

"Good luck," the man said, waving as Cain strolled out of the cage.

"Zip it, Randy," the guard barked, cuffing Cain and locking the cell back. He hauled him to an interrogation room where a man in a brown suit sat at a dingy table. The guard cuffed Cain to it after forcing him down into a thin metal chair. He left the room in silence, closing the door behind him. The room was dim and colder than the rest of the building with a large two-way mirror on one grimy wall. Everything there was designed to make him as uncomfortable as possible but a little dirt, a hard seat, and cool temperatures were nothing compared to the hells he'd been through. If they were looking to force a confession from him, they'd need to try a lot harder than 'uncomfortable'.

"Mr. Adamson," the man said, not looking up from his file. He whipped out a photograph and slid it in front of him. The image brought acid to the back of his throat. "Antoine Moreau's body washed up in front of St. Andrew's Castle a few hours ago. Scared the shit out of some tourists."

He couldn't keep the tears from coming, the sight of his lover's body gray and bloated, his lips blue and his eyes milky. He covered his mouth, swallowing a sob. After a moment, he cleared his throat and flipped the picture over, unable to look at it any longer. "Isn't Scotland a little out of your jurisdiction, detective?"

"Not when I get a call from Interpol. Now, based on your reaction to seeing that, I don't think you killed him."

"You don't?" His brows raised in surprise.

"I have a theory. You want to hear it?"

He nodded.

"I think it was her." He placed another photo in front of him, this one taken by a surveillance camera. He recognized the woman right away. Lilith. "This is Catriona Stewart, aka Cat. Twenty-nine years old from Aberdeen, Scotland, now residing in Edinburgh. A known sex worker with a rap sheet as long as my arm. Eight counts of petty theft, two counts of solicitation, three DUIs, and one count of kidnapping of a sheep."

"Did," he dipped his chin. "Did you say she kidnapped a sheep?"

"Never found the thing, either. Crazy broad, if you ask me."

He nodded in agreement.

"Now, according to witnesses, she beat the shit out of another woman and murdered her in your presence, is that right, Mr. Adamson?"

He thinned his lips.

"That's okay, we know she did it. One of the witnesses filmed it on their phones. In the video, we can see you and it looks like you tried to stop her. Is that true? Did you try to stop her?"

He shifted in his seat. "Well, yes but--"

"And, then you dragged her away but you didn't turn her in. Why is that, Mr. Adamson? Did she threaten you?"

"She has but--"

"Witnesses also say she and the victim were arguing just before the altercation. Fighting, actually, over you. Is that true? Were you and the victim, a Deirdra MacDonald an item?"

"Years ago, yes."

"Mm, hmm. So, we know she killed Deirdra. That's not in question. What I want to know is, did she also kill Antoine?"

"No," he told him without hesitation.

"You sure? Because by all accounts, you're an upstanding member of society. Business owner, real estate mogul, no priors. I don't like you for this but I'm loving her for it. Why are you protecting her? She your girlfriend?"

"Ex-wife, actually."

"Oh, I get it. She blackmailing you?"

"No."

"You sure about that because I have another theory."

"Do tell."

"See, I think she's the jealous type. Killed that girl because she's another ex of yours and she wanted you all to herself. When that wasn't enough to get you back, she threatened to out you."

"Out me?"

"Antoine was another of your exes, wasn't he? That's what his sister said."

"I'm not closeted, detective. I have no issue with anyone knowing who I'm seeing."

"What is it, then? Secret kid? Money laundering? Why won't you give her up? You really want to go down for something *she* did?"

"That's enough, Williams," another detective said, entering the room with heavy steps and a look of frustration. He was older than the other man, late forties, with a loosened tie and wrinkled blue suit. He had deep crow's feet and an unfortunate hairline, biracial with freckles and a thick mustache. Williams jumped at his voice so Cain surmised he must be his superior. "I'll take it from here."

He threw his hands up and stood. "Sorry, man," he said, giving Cain a look that said 'sorry, not sorry' and walking to the door. "I tried to help you."

The new detective sat down, lacing his fingers together on top of the file but not looking down at it. Instead, his eyes bore into Cain's as he sucked on his front teeth. They sat in silence for a moment while the detective inspected Cain's face.

"Do you have a question?"

"A few. Let's talk about your wife."

"Ex-wife."

"If you say so. How would you describe your relationship?"

"Volatile."

The detective laughed. "I can relate to that. But, that's what happens, isn't it? When there's passion."

"I suppose."

"She's a pretty girl. I can see how she hooked you."

"You should have seen her when we first met."

"Prettier?"

"Stunning."

"The kind of girl you'd do anything for, including lie to the police?"

"I haven't lied but if pressed, I wager I would, if the circumstances called for it."

"Why did you come here, Mr. Adamson?"

"Your subordinates didn't give me much choice."

"No, I mean to New York. You followed her here, didn't you?"

He didn't answer.

"It's all right, Mr. Adamson. We know she's in town."

He dropped his head. "Yes."

"The men she's with, do you believe them to be a threat to her?"

"Yes."

He stifled a laugh. "And, you thought you'd fly here and what? Save her?"

He looked him in the eye. "I have to try."

He sat back, dropping his hands to his lap. "Loyalty. I respect that, I do. One more question and we can move on. Do you still love your wife, Mr. Adamson?"

He slumped in his seat, his eyes falling to his cuffed wrists. "If I'm being honest, I hate myself for it but yes, I think there will always be a part of me that loves her."

"That's all I needed to hear." He flicked his fingers in Cain's direction, the cuffs unlocking as if by magic. Cain's eyes widened as the detective winked.

He stared as the man in front of him held his arms out to his sides, the mirror and lights shattering in a sea of glass and sparks. He sat dumbfounded and whispered, "Lilith."

"You didn't think I'd leave you here to rot, did you?" Within seconds, the room was filled with armed police officers, their guns pointed at Cain and Lilith, confused stares on all of their faces as they screamed at them to put their hands and heads on the table. "Boys, boys, why the aggression? Oh, I remember now. It's because you're afraid. Don't worry. I'll make it quick." She made a twisting motion with her hand, snapping all of their necks, their bodies crashing onto shards of broken glass. "Come, husband. We have much to do." She grabbed his hand and dragged him along as she made her escape, tossing officers aside with her mind on her way out.

Outside, a beat cop fired on them, clipping Lilith's shoulder and pissing her off. "Hey!" she shouted, holding the wound on her shoulder. "That was uncalled for." She snapped her wrist, the cop flying out of the parking lot and into traffic. She used her elbow to break the window of an empty squad car and unlocked the door. She got in the driver's side, Cain waiting for her to unlock the opposite door and hurrying in as soon as she did.

He took a breath, checking the mirrors to see if they were being followed as Lilith sped away. "While I appreciate the impromptu jailbreak, pilfering a police vehicle wasn't exactly discreet."

"Fear not, husband," she said, making a hard right onto Belt Parkway. "I have a plan."

Chapter 14

"**W**E'VE BEEN DRIVING AN awfully long time," Cain complained. "Are you sure you know where you're going?"

Heading south on Essex, she held tight to the steering wheel, her expression unbothered but her body language telling a different story. "I admit, I got a little turned around losing our tail but I know exactly where we are now."

"And, when did you learn to drive?"

She shrugged. "Never but this body's muscle memory has proven quite useful." She turned onto Canal, flashing a smile, her shoulders relaxing. "Almost there." She glanced over at him, her smile wide underneath her new body's mustache. "I knew you still loved me."

He rolled his eyes. "Don't let it go to your head."

"You were coming to save me. To protect me."

He sighed. "Not my smartest move."

"I was getting a little frustrated that it was taking so long but when I discovered you were being detained and that was the reason for your tardiness, I decided to forgive you."

"How big of you."

"It's the nicest thing anyone has ever done for me. I will not forget your kindness, husband. At my earliest convenience, I will scrub your name and likeness from all databases connected to the authorities as repayment for your chivalry."

"You can do that?"

She scoffed. "Of course. It's easy enough, just a few tweaks to my old forced loss of memory spell. I'll have it done by the time I return."

"Return?"

She parked in front of a building out of time, its ornate facade and huge arched windows out of place among its more modern surroundings. Its entrance was sealed with a metal gate covered in graffiti, the letters ABC in blue above it. "I need to ditch this vehicle *and* this body. It's so uncomfortable. Seriously, never again. Men are intolerably unpleasant to be inside of."

"That hasn't been my experience," he said, regretting it immediately. To his relief, she laughed.

She pinched his cheek and opened his door with her mind. "You're adorable when you joke. Now, get out."

"Excuse me?"

"Go in. You'll be safe here until I get back."

"And, how would you suggest I get inside?"

She waved her hand, revealing the building's original doors. "I tore off the fencing when I first arrived to make it easier for us to come and go but left the image. Wouldn't want to be disturbed, would we?"

Through the faded mirage, he caught a glimpse of two men pacing inside. They moved as if drunk, their tee shirts stained with black splatters. "Are those demons?"

"Yes, this is where I hide them. Don't worry, they've been instructed not to harm you."

He slammed the door. "As unimaginable as this sounds coming out of my mouth, I'd rather take my chances with you."

"Aw, that's sweet but really, you should--" She was interrupted by the sound of sirens, red and blue lights flashing four car lengths behind them. "Well, I can't leave you *now*, can I?" She peeled out, speeding down Canal to Allen to Pike.

"They're following us."

"I can see that, husband. Why do you think I'm driving so recklessly?"

"Turn off the headlights. They'll have a harder time seeing us in the dark."

She did as he suggested, weaving blindly through traffic as he nervously looked back to see the police a good distance behind them but still on their tail. When they hit the intersection at South St. she slammed on the brakes, Cain having to throw his hands against the dash to prevent from bashing his head on it. "*Now*, get out."

"We're still being followed," he argued.

"Not for long." She opened his door and nudged him to the opening. "Meet me at the theater."

He stumbled out. "Where are you going?"

"To ditch this body, like I said. Hurry, go before they get close enough to see you." The door closed and he stepped away, watching as she sped through the intersection, narrowly missing getting hit by another car. Two police cruisers followed, but as she flew over FDR, they stopped dead, most likely as surprised as Cain was to see her barrel straight into the East River.

"This crazy bitch," he muttered to himself, turning back to Pike and racing to avoid being discovered.

Arriving at the theater, he was greeted with snarls and contemptuous stares, Lilith's demons clearly displeased to see him there. They were everywhere, at least a hundred of them, splayed on broken seats and hanging off crumbling balconies, the stench of alcohol, sulfur, and piss permeating every inch of the room. At the far end was a stage, a severed head dripping gore on a pike at its center. He recognized it as belonging to Corson, the ringleader of the party of demons that had abducted Lilith back in Ur.

"She wanted to send a message," a thin demon in a white tee shirt told him, both of them captivated by the grotesque sight.

"And, it was received, I expect."

The demon nodded, black ooze dribbling from his nose. "I would never betray her but others needed reminding. There is a reason she is loved and feared in equal measure." He turned to face him, sniffing the air near his neck causing Cain to lurch back. "You do not fear her, only love...and hate. Two sides of the same coin, too hard for you to distinguish which is which."

"Son of Adam," another demon spat, his clothes doused in blood and his mouth missing several teeth.

"You know me?"

"Only stories, only myths. I remember your mother, though. She was quite a beauty."

His blood pressure spiked, his cheeks flushing with sudden rage. "I beg your pardon?"

"Do not be cross. I never touched her, only watched. Only spied. Eve of Eden, so supple. So soft. Nothing before had been so pretty as she. I could not help but linger. Stare. *Obsess.* You favor her more than your father. Lucky you."

In blind fury, he leaped upon him, forcing him to the ground, his hand on his throat and his eyes wild. "You will suffer for your disrespect."

"You must stop this, Son of Adam," the first demon said, nervously glancing around the room at the others, their eyes all trained on Cain, hisses and growls filling the putrid air. "Lilith will be livid."

"She can't hurt me. None of you can. No one can, not without hurting themselves."

"Myth," the choking demon grunted.

His lip twitched, even the muscles in his face tight with anger. "Care to test it?"

"I leave you alone for five minutes and you're already causing trouble?" Lilith said, gliding into the room in a new body, this one female with olive skin, curly, raven hair, and cloaked in a crimson pea coat. She looked to be in her mid-twenties with full, painted lips and large, brown eyes, remarkably similar to how she appeared when they'd first met.

"He offended me," he seethed, his grip tight on the demon's throat.

"Offended?" She stepped closer, placing a hand on his shoulder. "In what way?"

"Tell her." He removed his hand but stayed straddled on the demon's ribs.

"It was nothing. Please, my queen. I meant no offense."

"Yet, you offended. How?"

"It was innocent. I told him of his mother, how she was beautiful and sweet."

She cocked her head and folded her arms. "And?"

"Nothing, I swear it. Just that I would look on her from time to time."

She bit the inside of her lip and tapped her fingers on her arm. "When?"

"Well, when she lived, of course."

"Yes, obviously but *when?* Before or after she knew shame?"

"My queen?"

She threw her head back, letting out an exaggerated sigh of derision. "Was she clothed or not, you nitwit?"

"Well, no but--"

Cain strangled him again, this time with both hands, the vein in his forehead visibly throbbing.

"I should let him kill you," she said. "It is what you deserve. But, the truth of it is, I need soldiers. So," She took Cain by the shoulders and lifted him up, pulling him away as the demon coughed. The demon tried to stand but she held him down with the force of her mind.

"I will have my vengeance, witch!" Cain shouted, the room filling with gasps from the demons watching.

"Of course, darling but we mustn't be rash." She kicked around the rubble at her feet and knelt to pick up a shard of decades-old glass. "Here." She handed it to him and took a step back. "It was his eyes that gave offense, yes? Nothing more?"

"So he claims."

"I swear, my queen! I never lay a hand on the woman!" the demon said. "Not that one, anyhow."

She ran her fingers through Cain's wavy hair, petting him like a dog as he fumed. "Take one, husband."

"His eye?"

"Yes."

He glared down at him as the crowd erupted in gasps and chatter, his jaw rigid as he seethed. "It's not enough."

"And, what would be enough to appease you, my love?"

He thought for a moment, no punishment seeming sufficient. After a few seconds, he settled on, "*Both*."

"That won't do," she told him. "If he can not see, he can not fight."

"Fine." He squatted next to him, grabbing him by the chin. "Then, I'll take one eye," He plunged the shard into the demon's left eye socket, scraping around the edges as he screamed, severing the connective tissue and plucking the orb from his head, blood oozing down his cheek. "And, for his revolting words, I will have his tongue."

Screams of horror echoed through the crowd as he pried the demon's mouth open, Lilith's magic keeping him from defending himself. He sliced off the muscular organ in one swipe, blood spraying in his face as the crowd shrieked. Cain stood, dropping the glass and stepping aside, allowing Lilith to kneel next to the maimed demon.

"Yuhraq," she said, waving a hand over his blood-filled mouth. A muffled scream escaped his throat as his wound burned, cauterized by his queen's magic. She got to her feet, leaving her subordinate on the floor, his hands covering his face as he squealed. "Let this incident be a reminder since some of you have seemed to have forgotten," her voice boomed as she addressed the room. "Cain is my husband. My only love. In the hierarchy of the coming kingdom, he is above you. You will do as he commands unless his orders contradict my own. *You will show him respect.* Does anyone else need a lesson in decorum?"

The crowd was silent.

"Good." She faced Cain, her voice lowering. "Drop that thing, will you? It's disgusting."

He obliged, tossing the mutilated tongue at the whimpering demon's chest.

She looked him over, shaking her head. "You can't go around looking like that, can you?"

He looked down at his suit, doused in blood and gore, his hands sticky with it.

She passed her hand in front of him. "Yunazaf."

He held his palms in front of him, every bit of mess cleaned away by the witch's word.

"Sit tight," she told her minions."Refrain from drawing attention to yourselves. I will return as soon as I am able." She took Cain's hand and escorted him out of the building, two peas in a dark and wicked pod.

Chapter 15

ON A CHARTERED FLIGHT to Malaga, Cain settled in his seat, his eyelids drooping as he fought to keep them open, Lilith's new voice soothing but insistent.

"…One for me and one for Lucifer. Are you listening?"

He gave his head a shake. "I'm trying. What were you saying?"

"Ugh, you know how I hate repeating myself. All right, so there are two amulets. Well, three but we only need two. They function as a grounding element, keeping me and my brother in the bodies we've chosen so I can stay on Earth when the Gates close and Lucifer will be trapped, under a sleeping spell, and unable to come after me and my soldiers. One of them is in Spain."

"How can you be so sure?"

"Samael told me that my sister, Gabriel, dropped your daughter there when my father flooded a fifth of the planet to deal with the Nephilim scourge."

"That's true. I was surprised to see her that far from home. When I discovered what had taken place, I was convinced Elohim did it to rid the world of her spawn. It was years before I learned the truth. What does that have to do with the amulets?"

"Rumor has it, Allydia held on to some of my trinkets, bartered with them, sold them. I do not fault her for this. A girl's got to live and once things replaced God in the hearts of men, she had little choice. The amulet was what bought her a safe place to stay after my sister dumped her in the wilderness."

"That was a very long time ago. What makes you think it's still there?"

"The only people that would have accepted it as tender are witches and believe me, with as much power as those things hold, a coven would never give one of them up. Not voluntarily, anyway. It's there. I can feel it."

"And, if it's not?"

"I have a few more leads. Worry not, husband. I will free you of your curse, one way or another and we'll rule together, as it should have been from the beginning." She paused, looking him up and down, her brows furrowed. "You will age, wither. When you grow too old to satisfy me, will you be terribly offended if I take a lover? Or several?"

He ignored her question, too tired to feed her ego by feigning jealousy. "I told you, I have no interest in ruling."

"You say that now but I remember how proud you were of your city and you were right to be. The world had never seen such a magnificent metropolis. The architecture was unparalleled. Do you remember when you first brought me to see it? The pride on your face when you described each building, the gleam in your eye as we walked along the port and you told me of the trade routes you'd set up. You loved it there."

"And, then I had to leave it, for the second time."

She took his hand in hers and touched his cheek, turning his tired face to look him in the eye. "Never again, my love. I swear to you. I *will* relieve you of this wandering. If you do not wish for the weight of a crown, you can live out your days in the States. I will have it walled off from the rest of the world. You can live as you see fit, as Emperor or anonymously. Whatever you like." She kissed him gently, his body and his heart too fatigued to refuse her.

When they reached the hotel, Lilith insisted on sharing a room, convincing him with puppy eyes and logic. "You wouldn't want to leave me to own devices, would you?" she'd said. He absolutely did not, imagining the trouble she could get into, not that his presence seemed to tame her in the slightest. He only hoped he could keep her reined in enough that she wouldn't murder anyone else in public. The last thing he needed was to end up in another jail cell.

Sleep came quickly and lasted through the morning, Cain waking at just past noon, alone. "Bitch," he whispered to himself, taking his phone from the nightstand and checking her location. The app showed her at a shopping center not far from the hotel and as he wondered how she was shopping with no money, he noticed his wallet was missing from the nightstand where he'd left it. "*Bitch.*"

He took a shower and put on a pair of charcoal gray slacks and a white button-down, an outfit he'd had the concierge acquire for him the night before. His go-bag and briefcase were still in the New York police precinct and he had no idea how to get them back. Luckily, the officers who brought him in had forgotten to check his breast pockets so his wallet, phone, keys, notepad, and Lilith's mortar and pestle remained in his possession when he escaped. Regrettably, his clothing, toiletries, and preferred weapon were an ocean away. He'd just gotten the spike back after years of searching. Now, there was no telling how long it would be before he held it again.

"Finally," Lilith said, her voice bright as she came into the room, so much pep in her step, she was nearly skipping. She wore black, lace-up boots, light blue jeans, a white blouse, and a camel trench coat, clothes she didn't possess the night before. "I thought you'd never wake up. Here," She held out a sandwich wrapped in napkins which he took, just noticing the grumbling in his stomach. "They didn't have to-go boxes or anything and when I asked why the man glared like he wanted to spit on me so I gave him an aneurysm."

"We *have* had a discussion about avoiding the authorities from now on, yes?"

"I didn't touch him. From a bystander's point of view, he died of natural causes. Anyway, I already ate so finish that so we can go."

He swallowed a bite of his bocadillo, using the napkin to wipe away the olive oil dripping down his chin. "Go where?"

"Antequera. I got a lead on a coven there, supposedly the oldest in the country. If my amulet is still here, it is with them."

"How did you come by this information?" he asked, sitting on the edge of the bed.

Her lips turned up in a wistful smile. "Magic."

He blinked and shook his head, taking another large bite.

"Don't look at me like that. I didn't hear you complaining about my use of the dark arts when I broke you out of jail. Well, I did but that was mostly about my driving which I maintain was pretty spectacular given my inexperience."

He opened the mini-bar and took out a bottle of water, gulping down half of it and throwing his used napkins into a waste basket. He put his shoes on and grabbed his jacket, an exasperated sigh in his throat as he met her at the door. Opening it and stepping into the hallway, he paused to ask, "You said you ate?"

"Yes.

"Do I want to know what exactly you had for breakfast?"

She pressed her lips together, averting her gaze. "Probably not."

An hour later, they were standing in front of a two-story house on Juan Cascos Street, part brick, part bright white plaster with heavy, oak double doors and planters on the ground and hanging from the wrought iron terrace. The pots held a variety of colorful flowers that shouldn't have been thriving in the cooler weather, a tell-tale sign that a witch resided there.

"Irse!" a woman's voice shouted from inside.

"Rude," Lilith said, glancing at Cain and then glaring at the door. "We haven't even knocked, yet."

"Vete ahora demonio!"

Cain chuckled at Lilith's annoyed expression. "I don't think she likes you."

"Too bad." She splayed her fingers, the doors bursting open, the old woman inside scurrying back through the entry and into the sitting room.

"I don't have what you want!" the witch declared, backing herself into the ivory Sevilliana sofa, her ankles brushing the tasseled base as she fell into her seat. Her hand flew to her chest as they followed her, Cain hanging back while Lilith stood over her, the air in the room going thin.

"No, you do not." She bent down, hovering over the silver-haired woman. "But, you know where it is."

"I can't tell you," she said, her voice trembling. "It's far too dangerous, even for something like you."

"Something like me?"

Her breath quickened as she stared up at her, her lip quivering. "Diablo. Monstruo!"

"And, what makes you think that's what I am?"

"You radiate power, stronger than anything I've ever felt. And, you travel with him." She gestured to Cain who lifted his brows in surprise. "The immortal."

She laughed and whipped her head around. "You're famous."

"Do I know you?" he asked, trying to place her but coming up with nothing.

"My father owned a restaurant in La Rinconada. I saw you there as a child, then again more than thirty years later. You hadn't aged. You still haven't."

"Yes, he's very handsome for his age," Lilith quipped. "Now about my amulet..."

"*Your* amulet?"

"That's right." She sat next to her, the witch's mouth agape as she stared. Lilith leaned in, her voice low and her tone stern. "*Mine.*"

"I-it's impossible. It's not safe."

"I think I can handle it."

"No, you don't understand. In the fifteen hundreds, my ancestors were forced to leave their home in Catalonia and travel south. They hid their talismans and grimoires in the cave of El Toro. They remain there to this day."

She tilted her head and crossed her legs. "Why were they never retrieved?"

"We are too afraid." She nervously looked at Cain and back to Lilith. "You should be, too."

Lilith laughed again, tossing her hair over her shoulder. "Don't be absurd. I fear nothing."

"Then, you're not only a devil but a fool, as well. The caves are guarded," She swallowed hard, squeezing her hands in her lap. "By the wolves of Lobo Park."

Lilith and Cain exchanged glances of concern, the former then asking the question on both of their minds. "When you say wolves, do you mean wolves or...*wolves?*"

The look on her face told them all they needed to know but she offered a final warning, anyway. "You should stay away from that place. Nothing there can be worth the risk."

"I believe otherwise," she said, standing and planting herself in front of the aged witch. "Thank you for your help. How would like to be compensated?"

"Co--compensated?"

"What are you doing?" Cain asked, moving closer, his question more of a warning than an inquiry.

"She has done us a great service by providing valuable information. It's only right to repay her kindness, don't you agree?"

"Lilith,"

"Relax, husband. She is a fellow practitioner. I wouldn't hurt her unless she gave me cause and she has not. She has been most helpful and I wish to offer her something in return."

"I want nothing," she insisted. "Please, just go."

Lilith looked her up and down, her face brightening when she'd made a decision. "I know." She rubbed her hands together, leaning over. "What is your name?"

"Camila. Please," the woman whimpered. "I need nothing."

"What you need is irrelevant. What I am giving you is a gift." She flung her palms in front of the woman's face, slowly bringing them down to her neck, shoulders, chest, and abdomen. As she bent to reach her legs and feet, she declared, "Camila kana shaba."

Seconds later, as Lilith took a step back, weaving her arm through Cain's, the witch's appearance shifted. Her once gray hair was now a light, golden brown. Her eyes, previously sunken and hooded were now wide and sparkling. Her lips plumped and a rosy hue colored her cheeks, her wrinkles disappearing entirely. She held her hands in front of her, watching in astonishment as age spots faded and her nails, once yellowed and brittle, turned pink and glossy. She stood, tears brimming as she hopped from foot to foot. "What have you done?"

"I returned you to your true self. No need to thank me."

"But, I--this is too much. I don't deserve it."

"Why would you say that?"

"Because," She looked down at her body, clutching her new-ly-toned waist. "What I have given you, what I cursed you with, is a death sentence."

"Worry not, sister witch. Creatures such as us never truly die."

Chapter 16

A S NIGHT FELL ON the secluded Anequera park, Cain and Lilith sleuthed their way into areas closed off to tourists, creeping deep into the dense forest, neither of them dressed for such a hike, both too determined to care. After an hour of searching, they found the entrance to a series of caves, the two walking straight in without a moment's hesitation. Cell phone flashlights in hand, they explored the caverns, running into one dead end after another. Hours went by, their bodies growing tired and their patience wearing thin.

"How long must we endure this endless search before we admit that what you seek is not here?" Cain asked, leaning against the stone wall and then pulling his hand away, wiping the cool condensation on his jacket.

"It's here," she asserted. "It calls to me. Just a little further."

They kept going, eventually reaching a fork, two entrances to two caverns. They split up, Cain taking the right and Lilith the left. Alone in the dark, Cain began to regret venturing into these unknown chambers, the air getting thinner and thinner the deeper he went. The oxygen level was down to at least ten percent, given how hard he was having to breathe, his chest heaving by the time he got to a small opening at the end of the cavern. Sweat now dripping down the sides of his face, he peered in, the crevice too narrow for him to squeeze through.

"Lilith!" he shouted, his eyes becoming saucers as he looked at the hoard of books inside. Dozens of them in piles lined the walls while three massive oak trunks sat in the center, one of which had no lid, revealing a stash of silver and gold objects he couldn't quite make out. "Lilith, I believe I've found it!"

When no answer came, he doubled back, his vision getting blurry from lack of air. When he got to the fork, he called for her again. Still no answer. His flashlight went out, the phone's battery dying, his chance to call her's dying with it. "Son of a--" he muttered, putting it in his pocket, making sure to face the direction of the entrance. "Lilith!" he all but screamed, his deep voice echoing off the damp cave walls."I think I found it! Lilith!"

A high-pitched screech rang in the distance, hundreds of small voices sounding as one. They grew louder, the acoustics of the tunnels making it impossible for Cain to determine from which direction they were coming. "Damn it, witch, where are you?!"

The squeals intensified as a new sound joined them, the eerie flap of a thousand wings. His stomach dropped, the realization hitting him as he whispered, "Bats."

Suddenly, he was swarmed, hundreds of the spine-chilling creatures streaming into the space, their tiny claws scratching his face and neck, their wings smacking his head, back, and chest. He brought his jacket up over his head and ran, praying to a god he despised that he was going in the right direction. Sprinting through tunnel after tunnel, he thought he might pass out, the periphery of his vision sparkling with red and blue stars. Finally, after running for what felt like an eternity in the pitch, a gust of wind cooled his clammy face. Fresh air filled his lungs and in a few hope-filled minutes, he could see the light of the full moon brightening the mouth of the cave, the exit he'd been so desperate to find. The colony of bats flew ahead, leaving him behind in a flurry of shrieks.

He stumbled out of the cave, falling to the leaf-blanketed forest floor, his knees sinking slightly into the soft ground. He wiped his stinging face as he breathed, relieved sighs resounding through every exhale. After a brief rest, he got to his feet, turning back and cupping the sides of his mouth for better projection. "Lilith!" he shouted into the cave, hoping against hope that she could hear him. Still, no answer.

He leaned against a nearby boulder, rubbing his arms for warmth as he waited. She wouldn't leave without the amulet, or, if it wasn't there, without searching every inch of the underground network. His legs ached and his stomach rumbled. If she didn't emerge soon, he would have to leave her for a warm meal and a soft bed, an eventuality he would rather avoid. She wouldn't hurt him, not with the consequences to herself being seven times worse than any pain she could inflict, but she *would* complain...at length.

An abrupt but not entirely unexpected noise filled the chilly night air causing him to jump: the smooth, low howl of a wolf. He looked around but saw nothing, deciding the animal must have been a good distance away. "Come on, witch," he whispered, now trembling from cold and fear. Another wolf howled, this one in a higher pitch and from the other side of the woods. Soon, another howl and another, Cain's heart racing as nine voices came together to form a chorus. A set of glowing eyes appeared within the trees across from him, unblinking and unnerving. It was joined by another, this set more yellow than the first. To his left, another set appeared, then two more. He swallowed the lump in his throat, going over his options of which there were only two. He could dart back into the cave; it was only about six paces away from where he stood but if the beasts followed, he would be trapped and defenseless. Or, he could make a break for it, flee into the woods next to the cave, the only part of the forest not currently occupied by the menacing animals. From there, all he'd have to do is find a tree with low enough branches that he could climb. The latter seemed more practical, so after a deep breath, he darted to his right, reaching the tree line in a matter of seconds, the pack hot on his heels.

Leaves crunched and twigs snapped under his feet as the wolves gave chase, their snarls echoing in the night as he ran. His heart pounded like a drum, his skin slick with sweat, the forest growing darker the deeper he went. Soon, razor-sharp teeth nipped at the back of his legs which ached with fatigue, the adrenaline coursing through his veins the only thing keeping him going. Barks and growls rang out behind him as he tried not to panic, a task he found to be nearly impossible under the circumstances. More howls rang out, these from his right side. More wolves were coming.

His stomach cramped and his legs wobbled on the verge of giving out. He couldn't help but slow down, though he knew it would be the next death of him. Yes, he would come back, but that didn't mean he wanted to endure the pain of being torn apart by rabid animals.

In the near distance, he spotted an Iberian Holm oak with branches just low enough for him to reach. He sprinted toward it, gaining speed with his new-found hope. But, the beasts kept coming, the one in the lead pouncing on his back, digging its claws into the back of his neck. Searing pain spread down his back as the animal dragged him down, tearing his jacket to bloodied shreds. His face now in the dirt, two more tugged on his legs while the first clamped down on his neck, biting into him like a piece of meat which was all he was to them, their next meal wrapped in Brioni.

He tried to army crawl away but it was no use. His carotid had been severed. As he bled out, his limbs being chewed like drumsticks, he wondered if Lilith had found her precious amulet and if she did, if he would think it was worth this agony when he woke up.

Cain's eyes fluttered open, a starry sky through a canopy of trees the first thing he saw. Heat from a campfire warmed his skin as the scent of cooking meat lured his stomach to growl. Nude under an animal hide, he sat up to see a charred wolf carcass on a spit over the flames, chunks carved out of its hind and shoulders, its underbelly split open, its organs and entrails removed. In the trees, eight more wolves hung upside down with their throats slit. Perched on a hollow log was Lilith, her coat beneath her, a plate in her hands.

"What happened?" he asked, rubbing his throat, still feeling residual pain from the attack.

"Hmm?" She followed his gaze to the slaughtered wolves. "Oh. Shifters. Vicious ones."

"I hope you got what you needed."

"I did. Not before the shifters tore you to bits, though. If it makes you feel any better, I made them suffer for it." She took a plate of meat from the ground at her feet and handed it to him. "You should eat, then rest."

"Where did you get a plate out here?" he asked, popping a hunk of pre-cut meat into his mouth.

"It wasn't hard. A little guano, a simple spell."

"And, utensils?"

"What utensils?"

He glanced down at his plate, then back to her.

"Oh, no. I just tore it."

"I see." He took another bite, surprised that for a moment, he'd forgotten how strong she was.

"We'll sleep here and head back to the hotel in the morning for showers and breakfast. You're in no condition to travel."

He swallowed another piece of gamey wolf meat, ignoring the stringy texture as he was half-starved and ravenous. "Lilith," he said, his tone accusatory.

"Yes, darling?"

"Where are my clothes?"

"Just there," She pointed to another log on the opposite side of the fire where they sat neatly folded, his shoes on top of his jacket. "I mended them as they were in tatters, cleaned them of blood."

"With more of your spells?"

"Would you rather I left you with no way of covering yourself? *I* wouldn't mind but when we get back to town--"

"Thank you, Lilith," he said, unable to hide the sarcasm in his voice.

"You're most welcome."

They finished eating in silence, Cain finishing first despite Lilith's head start. He adjusted the hide and moved to stand but the sound of a plate shattering gave him pause.

"What are you doing?" she asked, getting to her feet, the shards of her dish in a heap underneath a nearby tree.

"Uh, getting dressed?"

"Absolutely not. I can not have you re-soiling the clothes I just cleansed by rolling around in the dirt as you sleep. They will stay where they are until morning."

He sighed in reluctant acceptance.

"It will be like old times. Do you remember, husband? The nights in the wild, nothing but grass beneath us, nothing but passion between us?"

He pinched the bridge of his nose, begging the memories not to come, his mind denying his request.

She snapped her fingers, her own clothes disappearing from her body and appearing in a pile next to his. "There's something about the forest, isn't there?" She stepped closer, leaves crackling under her bare feet. "A sensuality. The open air, the elements all around." She threw his covering back and set herself on his lap, guiding him inside. His breath hitched as she nibbled his earlobe before whispering, "Like freedom."

"Do you," he started, gliding his hands up her thighs to her backside, his eyes closing as he relented to his desires. "Do you truly believe my curse can be lifted?"

She bucked as she answered, her voice like a song in his ear. "Yes, my love. I will lift it, one way or another."

Cain woke with the first light of early morning, the sky above the trees an almost electric shade of blue. Birds chirped and dew moistened the earth, the night's fire nothing more than ash. Under the wolf hide, Lilith's head rested on his chest, his arm draped around her shoulder. It *was* like old times. The running, the killing, the fighting...the fucking. It was who they were when they were together; erotic, violent, and toxic. Part of him wanted to protect it, what they had. The sex, the violence. Even the death. Destructive as it was, it was their way of life.

He squeezed his eyes shut, screaming at himself internally, disgusted by his own thoughts. She was a malignancy, a cancer on his soul in need of removal. A creature of darkness he would be wise to put out of his mind. But, still, she was seeping back into his heart and that terrified him more than anything, including the idea of his curse remaining. He would have to find a way to free himself of her once she succeeded in lifting the curse, even if it meant he'd meet his true and final death.

Chapter 17

B ACK AT THE HOTEL, Lilith showered while Cain went over contracts on his phone, electronically signing each one and emailing his accountant instructing him to move all of his available cash to his American accounts. He then had a snack courtesy of the mini-bar and reflected on the previous night's happenings. Not the wolf attack; he never wanted to think about that again. Rather, the time he'd spent with his ex-wife. And, the time before that and the time before that. It was unfathomably stupid how he let her weasel her way back into his life and more so because what she offered was not at all what he wanted. He didn't wish to rule, to lord over people, demanding sacrifices and obedience like a god. Like his god. What he wanted was a normal life. A home. A family. The things Elohim's curse had taken from him.

Now, stewing in his resentments, pain erupted in his legs, like thousands of tiny bees jabbing him with their venomous stingers. "Shit," he grumbled, rushing to pack his things. "Lilith," he called, hearing that the shower had stopped running. "Lilith, we have to go!"

The agony spread fast, traveling up his body like wildfire. He doubled over, barely able to keep down the Marcona almonds and water he'd just consumed. Within seconds, he was on the floor, blood seeping from his nose and mouth as he crawled to the bathroom door. "Lilith," he gurgled, his voice nearly inaudible even to himself. He could hear her inside, chanting something he couldn't quite make out. "What are you doing?" he was able to ask loud enough to be heard, though the straining exacerbated his symptoms. He coughed up blood and bits of tissue, either from his esophagus or his lungs, he couldn't tell which. It didn't matter. Either way, if he couldn't get out of there and fast, he would die yet again.

"What I always do," she answered from the other side of the door. "Whatever I want."

"Lilith!"

"Just a little insurance policy. Nothing for you to concern yourself with."

He fell to his side, a crumpled heap in need of assistance but embarrassed. He hated that she would see him this way, weak and pathetic. It disgusted him to admit but no matter what she had done in the past, no matter how crazy she drove him or how crazy she was, he was still desperate for her approval.

His vision blurred as she finally opened the door holding a manila envelope. "Husband!" She put the paper to her lips and whispered, "lilaa wijhatik." The envelope disappeared as she knelt to touch his face. "Darling, do you need to leave?"

Unable to speak, he simply nodded, his eyes squeezed shut and his jaw clenched.

"All right," she said, standing and collecting their things. With hands full of suitcases and jackets, she went back to stand over him. "Can you touch me?"

Bells rang in his head as it pounded, sweat dripping from his forehead. He could hardly hear her through the incessant ringing. She sounded underwater and far away, her words only half recognizable.

"Touch me!" she shouted, scooting her foot next to his trembling hand.

With his last bit of energy, he slid his fingers up her shoe, getting a soft grip on her ankle.

"That's good, darling. Stay just like that. Alnaql alfadayiyu i niwzilanda."

He heard a *whoosh* then the sound of breaking waves. Underneath him, warm sand replaced the carpet of the hotel room floor, and stagnant air was made fresh, scented with ocean salt and gorse flowers. He opened his eyes, the pain in his head and body removed. "Where are we?" he asked, coughing one last time and swallowing the fluids lingering in his throat. He looked around the deserted beach, the setting sun over the water casting an orange hue over everything its light touched.

"They call it New Zealand now. Are you all right?"

He cleared his throat, stood, and brushed the sand from his clothes. "Fine. How did we come to be here?"

She shoved the bags into his arms, holding on to the jackets and checking his for her mortar and pestle. Finding it still in its place, she answered, "Teleportation spell."

He stared blankly.

"What?"

"You could do that this entire time?"

"Of course."

"Then, why have we been traveling by plane and train?"

She smiled sweetly. "To spend more time together, obviously."

"Fucking witch," he blurted, shaking his head.

"You said, 'thank you' wrong but you're welcome, all the same."

"What are we doing here?"

"Retrieving the second amulet." She looked out onto the ocean and took a deep breath, letting it out slowly. "Pretty."

"Are you sure it's here?"

"I distinctly remember sinking an island to hide it so yes, I'm fairly certain. Come. You need a proper meal and a rest. We'll begin our search tomorrow."

He reluctantly agreed, his legs like jelly a not-so-gentle reminder that, though technically immortal, he was susceptible to the weaknesses of being human.

They walked to the nearest hotel, a charming bed and breakfast overlooking Lake Rotorua, and had a dinner of fish and chips along with bottles of Speight's and pavlova for dessert. They then relaxed by the lake, enjoying the quiet and the cool breeze coming off the water. It was peaceful, a soothing respite from recent events that had consumed Cain's mind. He took an easy breath, closing his eyes, and leaning back in his white, plastic patio chair.

"Are you happy, my love?" he heard Lilith ask.

"No," he told her, opening his eyes and turning his head to look at her. "But, I'm closer than I have been in a while."

"Well, that's something, isn't it?"

He re-positioned himself, again closing his eyes and leaning his head back. "Yes, I suppose it is."

"Do you need sleep?"

"No." He got up, holding his hand out for her to take. "I just need this done."

She flashed a wide grin, taking his hand and standing in front of him. "To the woods, then."

In the forest, not far from the hotel, Lilith brushed her fingertips on every tree she passed, sniffing the air and listening to the sounds of the insects. Cain followed, swatting away mosquitoes and regretting not bringing his jacket.

"Why exactly do we need to be in the forest at this hour?" he grumbled, rubbing the cold from his arms.

"We're on the island I sank which means someone or *something* raised it. I need nature to find out who or what so I might ask where my amulet currently resides. It's here somewhere, I can feel it. I just need to tap into the island, listen for its past. Here." She stopped in a small clearing with a radius of only about forty-five degrees and got down on her knees, palms on the soft ground.

He warmed his arms again, holding back the bitchy tone he could hear creeping into his voice. "What on earth are you doing down there?"

She put her ear to the ground. "Listening." After a few moments, her features went tight, her head jolting from one side to the next as if she were watching a tennis match. "I can see them."

"Who?"

"A man. The one who raised the land from the depths. He hungered for immortality. For power. He deceived her, to his detriment."

"Again, who?"

"Her, she who waits. Her fury continues even still." She closed her eyes to speak directly to the enraged entity. "I've only come for what's mine. I will leave as soon as I have it." She grimaced, her teeth grinding. She looked up at him with slits for eyes. "She doesn't want to tell me."

"Why the hell not?"

She shook her head, her eyes widening with rage. Black lines formed on her skin, climbing up her arms to her shoulders.

Cain stood in shock, unsure if he should help her or flee. "What's happening?"

"I'm drawing on her power. If she does not give me what I want, *I will take it all.*"

Birds flew from the trees in a roar, the ground beneath them quaking. "Lilith," he said, holding onto a tree for support.

"She doesn't believe I can do what I say. I will show her who I am." She sunk her fingers deep into the dirt, the lines on her skin now spreading to her neck and cheeks. The ground shook harder, but she didn't stop. Instead, she dug deeper, swirling winds almost knocking Cain over. But Lilith remained unmoved, her voice booming in the night. "Show me!"

Wind howled through the trees, leaves and twigs flying in every direction, Cain doing what he could to shield his face while holding tight to the Rimu. As the sun rose, even the sky was affected by the witch's shenanigans, going from clear to overcast, thunder crashing as Lilith let out a wounded scream.

His heart jumped. In all the time they'd spent together, recently and in the past, he was sure he'd never seen her in pain. "Lilith!"

Another scream rang out, much lower in tone and coming from all around him. It wasn't Lilith's voice and it wasn't human. It was something else and it was everywhere.

The noise abruptly halted as did the earthquake and unnatural wind. Silence blanketed the forest as birds and bugs had long made their escape. Early morning sunlight filtered through the canopy as clouds receded marking the end of the battle, Cain's heart rate dropping back down to normal.

He raced to Lilith, the witch lying on the cool forest floor in nothing but a sundress, her shoes two feet away, presumably knocked off during the fight. Eyes closed and body limp, the dark lines traveled down her skin, to her hands then to the ground from where they came.

"Lilith," he said gently, kneeling next to her and tapping her cheek. "Lilith, are you all right?"

A weak smile crept up her lips. "You sound worried." She opened her eyes to look at him. "But, no need to fret. I'm fine *and* I know where my amulet is."

He helped her to her feet. "Good. I would hate for all that ruckus to have been for nothing."

"It's in the Waitomo Glowworm Caves."

"*Another* cave?" he complained.

"Yes, and apparently, it's a popular tourist attraction so, should we wait until nightfall when it's closed to the public or do we simply kill anyone who gets in our way? I'm fine with either option."

"I'm getting tired. We should probably wait."

She stuck out her lip in a pout. "Spoilsport. But, fine. It gives us some time." She reached for his belt, swiftly unbuckling it and yanking it away before going for his trousers.

He pushed her hands away. "I told you, I'm tired."

She scoffed. "You've never been too tired for me." She unzipped his pants and pressed against him, running a muddied finger down his stubbled cheek. "Do not refuse me, husband. I promise I'll be quick."

He grunted, his brain and body at odds, his breathing becoming so fast, he had to open his mouth.

She stood on her toes, licking his top lip, her voice quieting. "Up against a tree, like the old days." She brushed her lips against his, pulling his pants down just enough and raising her skirt to her hips. "Be with me." She grabbed his wrists, forcing his hands to her rear end. He couldn't help but clutch the ample flesh, grunting again but unable to back away. She lifted a leg, then the other, wrapping herself around him and kissing his neck. She slid herself up and down his disloyal member, Cain cursing its disobedience as it ached for more. "Do you want me to stop?"

This is the last time, he thought, sinking into her. "No."

She giggled as he spun them around, slamming her back into the tree he'd used for protection moments ago. "Good," she said between moans. "Because I wouldn't have."

He thrust harder, lecturing himself in his mind, his heart breaking with every pleasurable sensation. This had to end. It was tearing him apart. With labored breath, he hissed in her ear, "I still hate you."

She giggled again, running her fingers up the nape of his neck and grinding hard against him. "I know."

Chapter 18

T HAT NIGHT, ON A pilfered square stern canoe, the two floated on black water under a sea of shining blue, the cave ceiling and walls speckled with glowing gnat larvae. Cain shivered, bundling himself in his jacket while Lilith dragged her hand through the freezing water, admiring the small lights and humming to herself, her cheek resting on the gunnel. While cold, the evening's outing was so peaceful, if he wasn't stifling the urge to throw her over the edge of the boat, he might have confused it with a date.

"Are you sure it's here?" he asked. "We've been drifting for hours now."

"It's here, just a few feet ahead. She's warning me to turn back."

"The thing from before?" He scoffed. "You would think she'd have learned her lesson."

"She's cross with me for disturbing her. Says I should not have woken her. You know, I think she still doesn't know who I am. Shall I enlighten her?"

"You should get what you're after so we can leave this place. She almost killed you last time you tangled with her."

"She what?" She laughed, sitting upright. "My dear, sweet husband, this thing can not kill me any more than you can."

"Regardless, I'd like to get back to the hotel. It's rather cold in--"

"Shh. We're here."

He stopped the canoe, glancing around at the illuminated walls and spotting nothing resembling an amulet or place to hide one. "Where?"

"There's a crevice, only wide enough to fit a hand through."

He squinted, again checking the walls and finding nothing. "I don't see it."

"It's just there," she said, pointing to a spot in the water on the right side of the boat. "Be a dear and fetch it for me? I never learned to swim."

"You must be joking."

She shook her head.

"That water must be fifty degrees. I'll freeze."

She grazed his upper thigh, her eyes twinkling. "Then, when you return, I'll warm you."

He batted her hand away, staring daggers as he grunted.

"With a spell," she said with a laugh. "Please, darling. It's the only way." The boat rocked as a low rumble echoed through the cave. "Better hurry. Our friend is displeased."

"Ugh, *fine.*" He slipped out of his jacket and removed his shoes and socks. Peering into the abyss of pitch, he asked, "How will I see it?"

"Quite easily, I think." She scraped a handful of the glowing creatures from the wall and whispered to them, "Meaan." In her palm, they bound together forming a ball of bright, blue light. She offered it to him and he took it.

"Slimy," he said.

"Don't complain. They're aiding you. You should show them some respect."

"The bugs? Really?"

"They are part of the natural world, as are you. Do you feel so far removed from the earth your kind sprung from that you belittle others who did the same?"

He sighed, looking again to the depths below. "I feel far removed from everything on this planet. I'll be relieved and downright giddy when I am finally able to depart it for good."

Another quake wobbled the boat, this one stronger than the last. "Go, husband. I will keep our friend occupied."

Makeshift flashlight in hand, he sat on the edge then tossed himself over, regretting it as soon as the icy water hit his skin. His eyes stung as he peered through the frigid underground river, the crevice he was meant to find nowhere in sight. After a few minutes of searching, he popped up for a breath, gasping as he saw Lilith clinging to the cave ceiling, dark lines appearing on her arms.

"Quickly, husband! She threatens to harm you if we don't leave. I can hold her off but you must hurry."

The boat rocked with another quake, an eerie moan reverberating off the limestone walls. His teeth chattered and his lips turned blue, the strange entity a secondary priority as the cold stiffened his muscles. He dove again, swimming as fast as his aching body would let him. After about three minutes, he saw it, a crack in the rocky river floor. He swam closer, shining the glowworms over the crevice. There, mere inches away, was the sparkle of something hiding inside. He reached for it, but as his fingertips met the tarnished metal, a current swept him away, pushing him thirty feet and flipping him over. He scrambled to swim up to the surface before his air ran out, breaking through just as he thought he might pass out.

He looked around to see how far he had been flung and saw Lilith back in the canoe, lines all over her arms, neck, and face, her head back as she chanted something he couldn't hear. He swam toward her, disembodied shrieks piercing his ears as his muscles threatened to give out. When he reached the side of the boat, he took a deep breath, held it, and dove down, his burning eyes locked on the crevice several feet below. His periphery filled with glittering lights, his vision blurring. This was his last chance.

He plunged his rigid hand into the nook, forcing his fingers to wrap around the bronze bobble, every muscle in his body now cramping. He fought through the pain, yanking the amulet from its hiding place and making his ascent. But, as the light from the surface met his hopeful gaze, something caught his leg, pulling him back down.

With the amulet between his teeth, he shined his glowworm ball on his ankle but nothing was there. No animal, no seaweed. Just an invisible force that did not want him to leave with Lilith's amulet. He struggled against it but it was no use. Whatever this entity was, it had him dead to rights. At the bottom of the river, out of air and losing his sight, he took the trinket from his mouth and shoved it into his underwear, knowing that when his corpse floated to the top, it would still be there. Either, he would present it to Lilith when he woke or she, in her perversion, would find it there.

Water spilled from Cain's lungs as he coughed, his throat on fire and his head spinning. When he was done hacking up fluid, he rubbed his eyes, expecting to see Lilith next to him in the boat. Instead, he found Samael, sitting on the bow seat, dripping wet.

"Was I dead?"

"Only for a moment," the angel told him. "You mustn't tell my sister. She'll split this island in half to take her revenge."

"You...pulled me out? Gave me CPR?"

"Of course."

"But...why?"

He cocked his head. "I told you, my sister would kill everyone on this island if its witch had killed you, even temporarily."

In the distance, he heard Lilith shouting followed by a high-pitched howl, the canoe nearly tipping as a quake shook the cave. *That thing's a witch?"*

"Used to be."

He sat up, blanketing himself with his jacket. "Why aren't you helping Lilith?"

"Not my place. Besides, she can handle herself."

"She can, indeed."

Samael opened his palm, revealing the ancient amulet.

Cain was offended but not surprised. "You went into my--"

"What is it that you truly want, Son of Adam?"

"You know the answer to that."

"I thought I did. You told me you long for family and I believe you meant it but that's not really it, is it?"

He dropped his chin, chewing on the inside of his cheek.

"You long for death, don't you?"

He gave a small nod before lifting his eyes. "I confess, I am very tired."

The angel leaned in, the intensity of his stare bordering on violent. "Listen to me, Son of," he paused, his fierce eyes softening just a little. "*Cain*. Someday...*soon* I will deliver you to what comes next. You will know I'm coming and you will fear it but I *will* take you. You have my word." He placed the amulet in Cain's hand and sat back, watching as the immortal reacted.

He stared into the angel's impossibly strange and beautiful eyes, his heart dropping to his stomach and his voice barely above a whisper as he asked through chattering teeth, "Why do I believe you?"

"Husband!" Lilith shouted from somewhere in the distance.

"Remember," Samael said, holding an elegant finger to his lips. "Shh." With that, he was gone, disappearing in a blink once more.

He shook the encounter from his mind and called back, "I'm here!"

Another quake rocked the boat as shrill squeals bounced off the walls. He covered his ears, the high frequency causing them physical pain. From a cavern up ahead, he saw Lilith, crawling like a spider on the ceiling toward him. He got into his jacket, put his footwear back on, and hugged his arms for warmth, not that it helped.

She dropped into the boat, almost tipping it. "Are you all right?" she asked, cupping his face. "You're freezing. Come." She gripped his shoulders and recited the teleportation spell, blinking them away, leaving the island's witch to terrorize no one but the bioluminescent creatures that called the cave home.

Back at the hotel, Cain took a long, hot shower while Lilith watched, her prying eyes from across the room sending shivers up his spine even in the near-scalding water.

"Your body is as beautiful as ever, husband," she said, twirling her hair. "I wish I could give way to it once more but I really should be going."

"What?" He shut off the water and stepped out, wrapping a fluffy white towel around his waist. "Where?"

He followed her out of the bathroom where, on the nightstand, she displayed the two amulets and mortar and pestle. "I have everything I need, aside from an army, but I have feelers out for that. I need to go to New York for a meeting with a radio show host so hopefully, he can gather me recruits. Plus, my minions are there as is my brother. I must incapacitate him before he discovers them."

"What if Lucifer finds you before you find him?"

"He won't. Thanks to my decoy, I know exactly where he is."

A small earthquake shook the room, Cain's eyes widening while Lilith remained unfazed. "You're not going to handle that first?"

"I do not care to destroy Hine. I got what I was after." She put her things in a bag and threw on her jacket. "She's the island's problem now."

He lifted a brow, folding his arms and biting his lip. "There's something you're not telling me."

She smirked. "Isn't there always?"

"Yes, it's one of your least attractive qualities."

Her features scrunched. "Are you insulting me, husband?"

"Only if you find honesty insulting."

"I find *your tone* insulting. Honestly, I'm doing all of this for you. The least you could do is be nice."

"I'm not actually a nice person and I find pretending to be one is more exhausting than it's worth."

"Be that as it may,"

"And, let's be honest, shall we? What you're doing, building an army, disabling Lucifer, is *maybe* thirty percent for me, at most. What you want is power. It's what you've always wanted. It's *all* you've ever wanted."

She, too crossed her arms, a look of indignance on her face and a hint of hurt feelings in her voice. "That simply isn't true. Yes, I want power. I deserve it after what my father did to me. But, you," She stepped closer, cupping his face and running a thumb over his soft lips. "*You* are the reason for everything I do." She gave him a gentle kiss and picked up her bag. "I will see you later, husband." She recited the teleportation spell and just like that, she was gone.

Chapter 19

ON A PLANE TO New York, Cain sat quietly, thinking about everything that had happened over the last few weeks; Antoine's death, Samael's promise, and Lilith's return. Had Samael meant what he said about one day rescuing him from his perpetual existence? He'd certainly seemed sincere but if his research was to be believed, he was a bit unpredictable. Could he have been lying? Do angels lie?

Lilith never had, at least, not that he could recall. She hid things from him, and kept secrets, but never outright lied. It was one of the few things they'd agreed on and a lesson he'd passed to his children, one he'd learned the hard way: Anything else can be forgiven by a parent or a partner but lying is the worst thing one can do.

As for Antoine, he was still not fully recovered from his former lover's unfortunate passing. He thought he might never be. They'd only been together a short time but what they shared was real. He'd been one of his great loves and though brief, their relationship was the healthiest he'd ever experienced, second only to his first marriage. He wondered what became of Awan, how many lives she'd lived, and if she was now happy, safe in Heaven. He hoped so, for no one deserved paradise more.

He leaned his head back and closed his eyes, not entirely sure what the hell he was doing. Flying to New York, chasing after Lilith. It was ridiculous and masochistic, not to mention long. The fastest flight was over sixteen hours. He'd been sitting so long, his legs were beginning to cramp. He rubbed his thighs and berated himself in his mind. *What the hell are you doing? Stay away. Let her go.* But, he couldn't. No matter what she'd done, no matter how much he hated her, wanted to wrap his fingers around her throat and squeeze until her eyes popped out of her head like a stress toy, he couldn't help but miss her. Deep down, nauseating as it was, it was Lilith who was the true love of his life.

He tracked her phone to an ally in Manhattan, the pavement slick with an earlier rain. It was dark, the overcast blocking the moon's light. The air was thick with the stench of rotting food coming from a dumpster and as he crept toward it, a young girl peeked out from behind, a puzzled look on her fair face.

"Husband?" she asked, stepping fully into view. She was tiny, no more than 5'3", thin as a rail with flowing blond hair and cheeks so naturally pink, he could see their hue in the dim light above a service door. She looked young. Too young.

"Lilith?"

"What are you doing here? It's not safe."

"What have you done? What body is this?" He moved closer, his eyes falling to the unconscious man propped against the dumpster, his legs splayed in front of him and his blond hair disheveled. There was a tear in his shirt rimmed with blood but he saw no wound.

"Do you like it?" She twirled, her snow-white sun dress puffing out as she gleamed. "It's so much more comfortable." She hugged her arms. "Feels like home."

"It's obscene."

She threw her arms down at her sides. "Do you not desire it?"

He grimaced, shaking his head. "Absolutely not. You may choose to be in the body of a child but I do not."

"Well, that's unfortunate as I've already bound myself to it. It's all right. I'll just allow it to age and in a few years when the nations of the world bow to me, we will reunite. After all, 'always toward absent lovers love's tide stronger flows'."

"Did you just quote Propertius?"

"I did a lot of reading before I came to you. The Romans were exceedingly interesting. I'm sorry to have missed their empire. Was it as entertaining as history paints it?"

"Sometimes." He gestured toward the man on the cement. "Who is this, now?"

She flashed a toothy grin. "You don't recognize him? Of course, you don't. He's in a body you've never seen. Cain, darling, I present to you, a neutered Lucifer." She kicked him in the ribs and laughed. "Not actually neutered. I left his delicate bits alone. What I mean to say is, the threat of him has been neutralized."

His mouth gaped. She'd done it. She beat Lucifer.

"Don't look so surprised. My brother may be God's strongest but I'm his most crafty." She stiffened, her eyes saucering as her gaze darted to something behind him.

"What's wrong?"

"Shh." She grabbed him by the shoulders and pushed him behind the dumpster, forcing him down to a kneeling position and crouching next to him.

"What are you--"

"I said, shh." She peeked around the corner, Cain doing the same. At the entrance to the ally was a woman in her early to mid-thirties, with long, wavy brown hair, doe eyes, and high cheekbones. She wore a fitted leather jacket, dark wash skinny jeans, and shiny heeled boots.

"Who is that?" he whispered as the woman paused, then continued down the street.

She let out a relieved sigh and stood, offering a hand to help him up, which he ignored, getting to his feet on his own. "My sister, Gabriel. I didn't know she was in this city. She must be looking for me...or Lucifer. I'll have to be more careful with my comings and goings from now on." She furrowed her brows in annoyance. "She gets on my nerves." She relaxed her face and turned her attention back to Cain. "You should leave now, husband. If she recognizes you, she'll know I'm here, if she doesn't already."

"What are you hiding from me?" he blurted, unable to control his volume.

"*Shh*. Seriously. Do you want me to get sent back to the cage? If Gabriel finds Lucifer, she'll figure out a way to wake him and then they will come for me."

"*Lilith*,"

"Fine!" She scurried to the sidewalk, looking in the direction Gabriel was headed and walking back, her shoulders relaxed. "My sister isn't the only one that's made this city her home. Allydia is here, as well."

He gulped, the sound of his daughter's name on Lilith's lips reminding him just how much he loathed the witch. "I see."

"Vampires lurk around every corner, reporting to her. She is their queen. If you don't mind me saying, I'm very proud of her."

He cleared his throat, stifling the urge to slap her. "Yes, she's done quite well for herself, given her circumstances."

She took his hands, pleading with her eyes. "We could rule together, all of us, she with her vampires and us with our army. I know you blame me for the distance between you but I can fix it. Let me be a catalyst for reconciliation, a bridge connecting father and daughter. Think of it, husband. We could be a family again."

He dropped her hands. "My daughter was lost to me long ago and as I've told you repeatedly, I have no desire to rule."

She slouched, her disappointment turning to hope as she spoke. "Very well. Then, perhaps she and I will pick up where we left off.

The two of us had great fun before my brother spoiled everything."
She kicked Lucifer in the ribs again, harder this time. "Casting me
out. Locking me up like an animal. I would kill him but he'd just find
another body to climb into and I'd be right back where I started."

His mind swam with overwhelm. It was too much. The love, the
hate. The angels. The death. Between Lilith's antics and a city full of
vampires, Cain had had enough. "I'll go." He started to turn but she
pulled him back.

"But, just for now, yes?"

He nodded, knowing that even though he despised her, she'd
been right. He would never be free of her.

"While we're apart, would you be terribly offended if I indulged in
affairs of the extramarital variety?"

He let out an amused sigh. "Indulge in what, or whom, you like.
Just be discreet. We both know how overzealous you can get."

She gave him a wink. "No promises."

He took the first flight out of the city, his body aching and his mind
swirling. He made arrangements with his accountant to add Tamsen
Flagler, the girl Lilith was occupying, as a secondary signer to his
liquid accounts, giving her access to the money she'd need to hire
soldiers, bribe politicians, or whatever else she needed.

He landed in Chicago, heading straight for his North Lincoln Park
apartment. One of his more expensive homes, the price was well
worth it for the ambiance and classic architecture. There was nothing he liked more than a beautiful building.

He peeled off his jacket, more than ready for a shower and a nap. He moved through the entry to the living room, headed toward the hall when he spotted a package on the glass coffee table. Mail didn't come to this address as he hadn't lived there in years so this was a bit worrisome but he was too intrigued not to investigate. Worst-case scenario, it was a bomb or some sort of toxin. What was one more death in the grand scheme of things?

He picked up the box, perplexed by its lack of address or postage. Upon further inspection, he discovered it bore no tape. Instead, it was sealed by something unseen. He set it down, smacking his lips. "Magic."

He cut the box open using his keys, his eyes widening and brimming with grateful tears as he saw its contents, his briefcase. He took it out of its cardboard encasement and opened it up. There, nestled in its place, was his spike, a note on pink stationery resting on top of it that read:

Give to Caesar what belongs to Caesar

Love, L

Chapter 20

S AMAEL STROLLED THROUGH THE New York City hospital, unseen by anyone with human eyes. The emergency room bustled with bloodied gurneys carrying car crash and shooting victims, over-worked nurses, and doctors doing what they could to keep up, patients outnumbering them ten to one. In the last five minutes alone, Samael had ferried three people to the other side, one of them kicking and screaming, begging to stay long enough to say goodbye to her adult children. He'd ignored her request, it not being in his power to prolong life if God had commanded it be one's time to go. The mention of his father had soothed her, as it often did. People seemed comforted in their final moments to know there was something more, something bigger.

Coming upon a particular doctor, he cracked a smile, recognizing him as his brother, Raphael. He paused to watch him work, his patient ghost white from the loss of too much blood. He had several scrapes and scratches on his face and arms but his real problem was the gaping abdominal wound. A mess of blood, bile, and shredded internal organs, his injuries were fatal. However, the man wasn't on his list. He wasn't meant to die. But, from the looks of things, he was on his way out. Unless...

Raphael flung a blanket over the man's torso and slipped a hand underneath. No one else seemed to notice but Samael was pay-ing close attention, watching with interest as a pale glow showed through the white cotton covering. Slowly, color returned to the patient's face, the doctor letting out a breath Samael hadn't realized he'd been holding. The patient's eyes fluttered open, a tear streaking down to his temple as he lay motionless.

"You'll be fine," Raphael told him. "Just a few cuts and bruises."

Samael smiled again, making his way to the elevator. Once on the right floor, he beelined to the room he'd been looking for. No, it wasn't necessary for him to be there, but he felt it only right.

He entered the room, invisible to the nurse who changed the patient's IV bag. He moved around to the opposite side of the bed where he lay helpless, hooked up to beeping machines, a tube down his throat.

"This must be uncomfortable," he said, looking over his sleeping face and his chest, rising and falling with unnatural force, the machines doing the work of breathing for him. He'd be angry when he woke. Luckily, Samael would be back in Heaven long before, thereby avoiding any unpleasantness.

The nurse left, leaving the angel to gently push the patient's hair away from his face. He leaned down, whispering in his ear, knowing he couldn't hear him but wanting to tell him all the same, "One day, you will thank me for this, brother."

Samael returned, basking in Heaven's warmth and white light, God's ever-present hum filling him with peace and contentment. Rising to the Choir of the Seraphim, he reveled in the complete bliss, his burden behind him. Finally, and for the next two centuries, he was and would remain home.

"Sam," Michael said, forming in front of him in a sparkling fog.

"Michael. Good to see you."

"And, you. How is Lucifer?"

"Lonely."

"I'd expect as much. How does he look?"

He thought for a moment, the image of his brother in a hospital bed in his mind so disturbing, it was hard to put into words. But, one stuck out as the most accurate. "Weak."

He laughed. "There is a first for everything, is there not?"

"It appears so."

"And, Lilith?"

"In New York, as intended. Worry not, brother. Elohim's plans have been set in motion. I have no doubt the side of right will prevail."

He pat his back, a look of relief on his incandescent face. "Excellent work. Father will be pleased. And, what of the other?"

"Thanks to our unwitting sister, his destiny, too has been set."

Chapter 21

NAVID STUMBLED INTO HIS London flat, groggy from lack of sleep and painkillers. He dropped his mail on the coffee table and scratched at the bandage on his arm, his navy tee shirt stained with blood.

He collapsed on the couch, the room spinning, his head filled with cobwebs and Pen's words of warning. *You work too much. You don't sleep. Someday, it'll catch up to you.* She'd told him, repeatedly, to take a break. To take care of himself. Had he listened, he probably could have avoided being shot by a two-bit Younger. As it was, he'd been so focused on tracking the leader of the Mare Boys since he'd gotten back to town, he hadn't seen the member of a rival gang waiting to make a move on him. The two groups opened fire on one another and as he was ducking out to avoid being spotted, a stray bullet grazed his left bicep.

"Navid!" his girlfriend yelped, bursting into the flat, her lipstick smeared and her hair a mess. "Are you all right? Work called, said you'd been shot." She hurried to him, sitting next to him and inspecting his bandage.

"I'm fine. Nothing a little iodine and a handful of stitches couldn't fix. Stung like a mother, though." He looked her over, his heart sinking at the sight of her. "Where you comin' from, Pen?"

"I...nowhere. I was just..."

"*Pen,*"

She put her head down, biting her bottom lip and avoiding eye contact. "I--I'm sorry."

"Who was it, then?" he asked, his voice raised. "Was it Timothy? I've seen the way he looks at ya, all googly-eyed. He damn near drools."

"No, not Timothy," she answered, not looking up.

"Caleb, then? Or that barista that gives you free coffee on Wednesdays?"

"No, it's no one you know.'

"Give me a name, Pen."

Her eyes flicked to him, her voice trembling. "You're not thinkin' about doin' somethin' crazy, are ya?"

"Course not. I'd just like to know which tosser you deemed fit to fuck me over for."

She shook her head. "I didn't mean to," she wiped away a stray tear. "I didn't want to hurt you."

"You thought I wouldn't find out? *I'm a detective, Pen*. You can only hide things from me for so long."

"It was Robert, okay? Are you happy?"

"Happy's not quite the word I'd put on it, no. And, *Robert?* The wanker you told to piss off a month before we hooked up?"

"Yes."

"The one you said was, and I quote, 'hung like a toddler with an IQ to match'?"

"Not my proudest moment but, yeah."

"You mean to tell me, while I was out getting shot at, you were off bangin' it out with a tiny-dicked, dumb-as-rocks, supermarket cashier from Lewisham? Well, that's just perfect, innit? A shitty end to a shitty night."

"Shitty relationship," she muttered under her breath.

"What's that?"

"Oh, come on, Navid. You know things have been crap for the last...forever. You never stop workin' long enough to have a proper night out. I'd settle for a twenty-minute conversation but you're not exactly handin' those out, either."

"You're blamin' you sluttin' in up with your ex on me not givin' you enough attention? That's just fine. Whatever helps ya sleep at night."

"I'm just tryin' to explain--"

"Just go."

She slumped her shoulders, shook her head again, sighed, and stood. When she reached for the door, Navid called her back. "And, Pen,"

She turned, brushing away another tear, a glint of hope in her eyes.

"Don't bother comin' back, yeah?"

Her eyes fell as she nodded, leaving the flat and closing the door behind her.

He took a few deep breaths, blowing them out his mouth as he tried to keep his hands from shaking. They'd only been together less than a year but they'd been friends since he joined the force. He wondered if someday they'd be friends again, or if he'd resent her too much. In that moment, he couldn't see past his pain, thinking he'd never be able to look at her the same way again. She'd forever be the girl that cheated on him. The girl that broke his heart.

To distract himself, he rifled through his mail, tossing bills and adverts back without opening them. At the bottom of the pile was a 5x7 manila envelope with no address or postage. "Must've been left by a neighbor," he told himself, ripping it open, too drugged and enraged to question it further. Inside, he found a few crumpled leaves, a blood-stained tissue, and two locks of hair tied together with a ribbon, one slightly darker than the other. "Ew." He didn't touch the contents, but he couldn't escape the cloud of perfume that floated from the herbs. He sneezed then shuffled to the kitchen and dropped the envelope in the waste bin. "Pranks."

He sat back on the sofa, shivering as a cool breeze from nowhere prickled his skin. He turned on the telly, deciding a bit of mindless relaxation was just what the doctor ordered, given the night's events and his intoxicated condition. He sat for a while, on the verge of falling asleep when the hairs on the back of his neck stood on end, another mysterious draft giving him chills.

BOUND BY BLOOD

Chapter 1

"YOU'LL HAVE TO DO better than that, boys," Navid taunted, hands tied with twine behind the back of the chair he sat on, blood dribbling from a cut above his eye. The dim warehouse he'd been dragged to was hot for June even with a row of ceiling fans whirring above. Crates of stolen goods lined the wall behind him while two roadmen stood guard at the entrance, their presumed leader rubbing his bloodied fist. He hit him again, dull pain spreading through Navid's jaw. He laughed, eyes twinkling as he looked up at his captor.

"What's wrong with ya?" the twenty-something-year-old criminal asked, blond brows furrowed in bewilderment. "Takin' a punch is one thing but I think you enjoy gettin' knocked about. You're sick, you are." He hit him again, this time bloodying his lip.

"I don't *like* it," he told him, licking away the blood. "But, when you've seen the things I have, been properly tortured, gettin' roughed up by you lot is a day at the park. Feels like love taps."

The two at the door chuckled, the leader fuming. "You think that's funny, do ya?" he barked at them, turning his head. "Either of you want to have a crack?"

They held their hands, shaking their hands. "Sorry, boss," the one on the left said.

The other one chimed in, "Yeah, no disrespect."

Preoccupied with bickering with and scolding his underlings, the leader didn't notice Navid wriggling out of his restraints. Hands now free, he stayed put, waiting for his opportunity to pounce.

"So, you're a comedian as well as a scuffer." He bent down, his face mere inches from Navid's. He readied his fists and stared into his eyes. "Tell me a joke, funny man."

"All right." Navid sat back, rubbing his wedding band with his thumb for luck. "What did the knuckles say to the door?"

"Can you believe this guy?" the leader asked the others. He turned his face back to his prisoner. "Fine, I'll play along. What did the knuckles say?"

He pressed his tongue to the inside of his cheek, smiled, and winked. "Bang." With all his might, he slammed his forehead into the man's nose, knocking him back, his face covered in blood. He leaped from his seat, kicking him in the diaphragm, forcing the air from his lungs. He pulled his legs up in a fetal position and held his broken nose while Navid stepped over him, the two at the door scrambling to get their knives ready.

"Don't you move, pig!" the one on the left said, a warning Navid chose to ignore. He barreled toward him as he raised the twelve-inch blade, dropping down and sliding the last few centimeters, and punching him in the balls. The roadman fell, dropping the knife and coughing while Navid swept the second man's leg, stood, and stomped on his gut.

"If you were teenagers, you'd have an excuse for bein' dumb as shit," he told them, kicking the knife away and using the twine that had bound him to tie together the leader's hands. "As it is, you're all just a gaggle of buffoons, holdin' up tourists and doin' the Mare's bidding."

The man to his left made a break for the door, but he caught him by the hair, pulled him back, and slammed his head into the wall, knocking him out cold. "See what I mean?" he said to the criminal on his right who lay clutching his stomach and catching his breath. "Stupid."

"Bright enough to catch you spyin'," the leader said from the concrete floor.

"You think that was you?" He laughed again. *"I let you catch me."*

"Bullshit."

"You don't think so? Look around."

The three roadmen glanced around the warehouse.

"You brought me right to one of the Mare stash houses. There are a couple hundred thousand pounds of stolen items in here, at least. With your boss in the clink, it'll be real easy to slip you in a cell, nice and quiet, and send a of couple bobbies out for a sting."

"You're dead," the leader spat, sitting up, struggling to free himself and failing miserably. "You hear me, pig? *Dead.*"

"Threatening an officer," He wagged his finger and clicked his tongue. "Not smart, bruv."

"Not smart at all," his superior said, leading a group of bobbies into the warehouse. The men were cuffed and hauled away, muttering more threats and obscenities as they went. "You all right?" she asked, tilting his chin up to get a better look at his battered face.

"I'm fine, Pen," he said, gently pushing her hand away. "Just make sure the charges stick, yeah?"

"You know I will."

⁂

"Umyeni!" Phindi yelped as Navid walked in the door of their London flat, shuffling to him as quickly as she could. She touched his cheek as she examined his injuries. "What's happened?"

"Just work stuff, love." He kissed her forehead. "Nothin' to worry over. And how's little man?" He placed a hand on her pregnant belly.

"Big."

He chuckled. "Just six weeks left."

"I am counting the days, believe me. I haven't been this tired and uncomfortable since eighteen seventy-nine."

"I'll never get used to you sayin' stuff like that."

"Have you thought more about what I said?"

He sighed. "This again?"

"Yes, this again. Look at your face!"

"I'm all right."

"You call beaten and bloodied all right?"

He sank into the sofa, closing his eyes in relief before addressing her again as she sat. "All in a day's work."

"Hence my concern."

"I'm not movin' to the States, love. My job is here."

"Your job is the problem. How many times have you come home with one injury or another?"

The real answer was more times than she knew about so he kept his mouth shut.

"A black eye here, a split lip there, not to mention the fractured collarbone last year and the cracked ribs a few months before that. How many near misses in gun fights? How many--"

"I hear what you're sayin', love but it's part of the job. I catch criminals, get them off the streets. It's for the public good."

"And, what about what's good for me, hmm? And Thando?"

"I never approved that name."

"It means love."

"So does Aziz."

"That means beloved, not love. It is entirely different."

"Is it, though?"

"We can have that argument later. My point is, every day when you leave for work, I worry. Every time the phone rings, I think it is someone calling to tell me that you've perished. I wait by the door if you are even a minute late, pacing in front of it like a mad woman. It is too much stress."

He held her hand, looking her in the eye. "I'm sorry, love. I know how hard it must be for you, but--"

"You do not know," she asserted, yanking her hand away. "You can not because if you could, you would not put me through it day in and day out. I admit, I find your strength and aptitude for close combat alluring, but sexy as it is, it is not conducive to a healthy family. I need you alive, Navid." She rested her hand on her belly. "We both do." She hoisted herself up and waddled to the kitchen, leaving him feeling frustrated and guilty.

"And, what would we do for money?" he asked, getting up and meeting her in front of the stove where she fluffed a pot of phutu.

She removed the pan from the heat and turned to face him. "We could live comfortably for a couple of years on the money I made selling the gym."

"And, then? You'll be home with the baby and I'll have to work to take care of you both and this, fightin' crime, lockin' criminals away, it's all I know how to do."

"The queen said--"

"I'm not takin' Gran's money, Phin. It's not right. She's my elder, yeah? I should be takin' care of her, not the other way 'round."

"She doesn't need taking care of, she is wealthy beyond--"

"That's not the point, is it? It's a matter of honor and respect."

She snickered, her fingers to her lips.

"What?"

"Nothing, it is just," She laughed again. "If you wish to show Allydia respect, do not let her hear you call her 'elder'."

He, too chuckled. "That's good advice."

"Best I ever gave you, next to *quit your job*."

He sighed, dropping his chin as she got dinner ready. Deep down, he knew she was right, knew he was acting selfishly by doing the work he loved. But, it was who he was, an officer of justice, a righter of wrongs. It was what he was born to do. How could he give it up?

Chapter 2

T HE NEXT DAY AT the station, Navid drank heavily sugared coffee from a paper to-go cup and considered Phindi's request. Sitting at his desk, elbow on the wood and cheek resting on his fist, he thought about his wife, worried, anxious, and tired of it. She wouldn't put up with it much longer, he could feel it.

"Parsi," Pen called from her office. He looked up to see her waving him in.

"Yeah, Pen?" he said, following her inside.

She closed the door and the blinds. "Sit down, Navid."

He remained standing. "What's wrong?"

She sighed, walking around her desk and sitting. "It's Duncan Lawrence."

"If you're tellin' me he's dead, that's no reason for that scowl on your face. That's reason to celebrate."

"Believe me, I wish he was dead." She slid a file across the desk. "He's getting out."

"What?!" He snatched the file, opened it, and read in disbelief. "Are you fuckin' serious, Pen?"

"As a heart attack."

"How could this happen?"

"You got me. They're citing ECSL but he's got way more than seventy days left."

"ECSL? That's bullshit."

"I know."

"Is there anything we can do?"

She shook her head, lips pursed. "Not a goddamn thing."

He slammed the file on the desk and paced for a few seconds, arms crossed and fuming.

"He's askin' to see you."

"Lawrence? What for?"

"To gloat, I assume. You shouldn't go."

"Probably not."

She sighed again, rolling her eyes. "But, you're going to, aren't you?"

"I might."

"Navid,"

"Not to cause trouble. Just to let him know I'll be watchin'."

"Not the call I'd make but you're gonna do what you're gonna do."

"I can't just sit by and do nothin'."

"Then, speak to his PO. Tell him to keep an extra eye on him."

"Who's his PO?"

She bit her lip.

"Who, Pen?"

She cleared her throat before answering, "Charlie."

"*Charlie?* You've got to be kidding me."

"I know."

"He's the most lenient, half-assed PO in the city."

"I know."

"This stinks, Pen. Smells like a conspiracy."

"Shh." She looked over his shoulder toward the door. "Whisper when you say stuff like that in here."

"He's got someone on the payroll, doesn't he?"

"I don't know. I assume but I can't figure who."

"Someone up in rank. A judge?"

"That's my guess but I can't prove it."

"Fuckin' hell."

"I'm looking into it.'

"Yeah, well, you do that. I'm gonna pay ol' Charlie a visit."

Navid walked to the probation center on St. John, muttering angry obscenities as he went. Once in the building, he headed for Charlie Evans' office, a tiny room cluttered with boxes of files in need of digitization and a dying ficus in the corner behind the desk. It reeked of smoke, Charlie putting out his cigarette and spraying room deodorizer upon seeing the detective.

"Still ignoring the smokin' ban, I see," he said, closing the door behind him.

"It's a private office. Shouldn't be a bloody crime."

"You're still protesting? It's been eighteen years, mate. Maybe time to admit defeat."

The older man leaned back in his chair, the light from the window behind him glaring off his scalp, his sad comb-over more embarrassing than helpful. His gut hung over his belt as the buttons of his shirt held on for dear life, a shadow on his brown slacks looking more like a stain. "You gonna turn me in, detective?"

"I could."

"Eh, what's another fifty quid in the grand scheme of things? What brings you by?"

"You got a new client getting out tomorrow."

"Oh, yeah. The Mare Boys' ringleader." He sat forward, shaking his head. "I can't believe they're letting him go."

"Any idea why they are?"

"Not the foggiest. They're claiming ECSL but he had six more years. Doesn't track if you ask me."

"Me, neither. So you'll keep a close eye, yeah?"

"I'll do my best."

"I'm gonna need you to do better than that, Charlie. No offense, but you're not exactly by the book."

"Now, wait a minute, Parsi,"

"I'm not insultin' ya, just sayin',"

"You're sayin' I don't do my job?"

"All I mean is, you're not exactly a hard-ass."

"Oh, so, because I don't get my panties in a twist over every little petty offense, I'm a pushover?"

"I'm not sayin' that."

"Listen to me, kid, when you've done this job for as long as I have, there are some things that just aren't worth the hassle. If I catch a guy snortin' coke but he's not selling it, not a danger to anyone but himself, I'm not inclined to ruin his life, especially when doin' it would be a mountain of paperwork for me. Look around. I've got enough to deal with."

"So, you look the other way because you're lazy, not because you're bein' paid off?"

His eyes became slits. "What exactly are you accusing me of, Parsi?"

He let out an exasperated sigh and rolled his neck. "Nothin' Charlie. I just want to make sure Lawrence is properly supervised, all right? He's not a petty thief or some poor bloke that got addicted to somethin'. He's a murderer, yeah? The head of a street gang."

"You think I don't know that?"

"All I'm sayin' is, I put a lot of work in takin' him down. Years of my life. I want to make sure he doesn't go right back to his old ways and if he does, I want him locked back up."

"I know how to do my job, Parsi."

He stood. "I'm not sayin' you don't. I'm sayin'," He moved to the edge of the desk, his expression and tone going cold. "If I find out you're slacking on this, you'll have bigger problems than a public smoking fine."

"Are you threatenin' me?"

"No threats." He turned to go. "Just statin' facts."

Walking back to the station, he debated whether or not to visit Duncan in prison. On one hand, he'd love to put the fear of God in him, tell him he would make sure he goes right back in if he so much as gets a parking ticket. But, those threats would be empty. Someone at the top was corrupt and he had a feeling that no matter what Duncan Lawrence did, he'd get away with it. The best he could hope for now was for one of his goons to turn on him, maybe kill him. He shook the thought from his mind. It was sick. He didn't want to be that person, the kind that wishes for people's deaths, even if they are criminals. But, there was a part of him that thought, *knew* the world would be a much safer place without Duncan Lawrence in it.

Chapter 3

A FTER HIS ESSENTIALLY USELESS conversation with Charlie, Navid met up with an informant in the car park of a council estate. If he couldn't trust Duncan's PO to keep him in line, he at least wanted to be kept in the loop of what he was up to.

"It's kind of out in the open, innit?" his informant said, taking a drag from his cigarette.

"You want me to rough you up a bit? Make like I'm givin' you a hard time?"

He took a small step back. "Nah, mate. That's all right." He glanced around, his tone calm but his mannerisms and facial expressions giving him away. He was nervous and for good reason. If anyone saw them together, he'd be made as a rat and that was an unforgivable offense as far the Mare Boys were concerned.

"Look, I'm sorry for draggin' you out here, yeah, but I've got no time to waste. Duncan Lawerence is getting out tomorrow."

"Yeah, I heard. Everyone's talkin' 'bout it."

"You know anything about how it's happening?"

He shook his head. "Not specifics but word is he's got friends in high places. *Real high*."

"Any idea who?"

"No, but it's more than one. I heard someone say he's got six judges and dozens of peelers on his payroll. At this point, it wouldn't surprise me if he had the bloody king doin' his dirty work."

"Fuck all." Navid sighed in frustration. The corruption was more widespread than he thought. Duncan Lawrence was just the tip of the crooked iceberg.

"You know he's comin' for ya, right?"

He rolled his eyes. "Someone always is."

"No, mate, I'm serious. He's straight gunnin' for you. If I were you, I'd get out of town before he's out of the clink."

"I'll be all right. You just let me know if you hear of him doin' anything sketch when he gets out, yeah?"

"Yeah." He glanced around again, took a few steps back, and dropped his cigarette, putting it out with his shoe. "Watch your back, though."

The informant turned, making it three steps before the sound of shots rang out, a bullet hitting him in the temple. By the time his knees hit the pavement, he was already dead.

"Shit," Navid muttered, pulling his weapon and taking shelter in the entrance of the building's parking garage. More shots came, these hitting the ground where he'd been standing. From their trajectory, he knew the shooter was in the building, at least four stories up. He'd never be able to search every flat alone before the shooter got away. He took his Tetra from his hip and called for backup.

After a few seconds, the shooting stopped. The gunman must have seen where he'd ducked into. It would've been impossible for them not to. With eyes glued to the car park he waited, jaw tight and gun cocked. Minutes went by, the anticipation driving him crazy. *Come out already,* he thought, watching every door for signs of movement. Finally, one opened, a man in a mask strolling out. They locked eyes, guns pointed at one another. "Hands up!" Navid shouted. The masked man stopped abruptly not five feet from him, kneeling to place his weapon on the cement.

Suddenly, Navid was hit from behind, the dull *thwack* of a tire iron hitting his back as loud in his ears as the gunshots. He went down, the air knocked out of him.

"Duncan sends his regards," the gunman in front of him said, reaching again for his weapon. Luckily for Navid, he'd never dropped his so, ignoring whoever was behind him, he took aim at the man's ankle and pulled the trigger. He yelped, falling to his backside.

"Oh, you'll pay for that, mate," a man behind him said. He turned to face him, a heavy-set ginger in his mid-twenties with an unkempt beard and bloodshot eyes. As he lifted the crowbar to hit him again, Navid donkey-kicked his kneecap, shattering the bone. He dropped, screaming in pain as the gunman took aim once more.

Navid darted to the opposite side of the garage, both men now in front of him as he caught his breath. "That the best you've got?" he taunted, his weapon pointed at the masked gunman, both of his assailants scooting on the ground, unable to stand.

"You should let us do you in now, Parsi," the one with the crowbar warned. "It'll be easier on ya."

"Easier?"

"Yeah, mate," the other man said. "Boss gets out tomorrow and he's made it real clear he wants you off the map. If we ain't able to get the job done, he's gonna do it himself and I'm tellin' ya, that's not a fight you want to have."

"I don't know. I'm pretty scrappy."

"You're stupid is what you are," the bearded man said. "Goin' after someone like him. He's everywhere, mate. Got his fingers in all the pots. You're so worried about justice getting done you didn't consider the cost."

"The cost?" Navid asked, head tilted in the direction of the sound of sirens approaching. "Looks to me like you're the ones payin' a price."

They looked at each other, the signs of anxiety clear on their faces.

"Can't run, can't shoot me without getting pinned for murdering an officer. Nowhere to go but where you belong." Holding his gun with one hand, he used the other to get his cuffs from his belt. He slid them over to the man with the crowbar who looked down at them with a puzzled expression.

"Cuff your friend," he told him.

"You off your trolley?"

"Trust me, boys, it's better for ya if you're not pointin' a weapon at a detective when the bobbies pull up."

The man with the gun shook his head.

"What's it gonna be, red beard? You've got about five seconds to make a decision."

"I--"

But, before he could finish his thought, the sound of tires screeching made him jump.

Navid smacked his lips. "Too late."

Four officers rushed in, barking at them to put their hands on their heads. Navid waited until they were cuffed before holstering his weapon and retrieving his handcuffs. "I tried to help you boys out."

"They never listen, do they, Parsi?" one of the bobbies said, hauling the bearded man out of the garage.

"Nope, they never do."

"You're gonna wish it'd been us!" the man with the blown-out ankle called as he was dragged into a patrol car.

Navid shook his head, trying to reach behind him to rub his aching back. He watched as the criminals were driven away and his informant's body was loaded into the back of a coroner's ambulance, guilt gripping him like a vise. He shouldn't have met him there, out in the open like that. It was a rookie move. He'd let his hatred of Duncan Lawrence cloud his judgment and he'd carry the burden of his informant's death with him for the rest of his life.

Back at the precinct, Pen gave him another lecture about getting into scrapes without backup, being too focused on the job, and not looking out for himself. Her usual spiel. He ignored her, his mind still on the murdered informant. Did he have a wife? Kids? Who would be affected by his death? Would anyone miss him? Why had he been so stupid? He never should have met him there. He knew better. It was his fault. A relatively innocent man was dead and it was all his fault.

"Are you listenin', Navid?"

He looked up as if being woken from a dream. "Yeah." He cleared his throat and sat up in his seat. "Yeah, I hear you, Pen."

"Do you? Because this is the what, seventh time this year you've been in here with one injury or another? You're not thinking."

"I am thinkin'," he defended. "I'm thinkin' 'bout how to put these criminals away, get 'em off the streets. I'm thinkin' this is what I do and I'm good at it, yeah? Say what you want but I always get the job done."

She crossed her arms and sat back, her lips thin with disappointment.

His stomach dropped. "What?"

"You're not gonna like it."

"What is it, Pen?"

She leaned forward, hands clasped on her desk. "Those blokes we picked up today,"

"What about them?"

"They're sayin' they have no ties to Lawrence."

"What?"

"Pretendin' they've never even heard of him."

"You know that's bullshit, right?"

"Obviously. I'm not a moron. They'll be charged with murder, assault of an officer, attempted murder of an officer, plus an illegal weapons charge. But, aside from what you said in your report, there's nothin' to connect them to Lawrence. They'll go away for a long time but..."

"Duncan will still get out."

"Yeah."

They sat in mutual discontentment, rage filling the room like air freshener. It was infuriating, the lies of two killers allowing Lawrence to once again escape justice. "I'm not havin' it," he declared, getting to his feet.

"What do you mean?"

"I don't know. I don't know what I mean but this isn't right. This isn't what this place stands for, lettin' people like him run 'round doin' as they like, killin' and robbin'. We're supposed to protect people from thugs like him."

"You're right. But, our hands are tied, aren't they?"

He grasped the doorknob, yanking the office door open, and storming out. "For now."

Chapter 4

T HE NEXT DAY, PEN dumped a month's worth of old paperwork on him, chaining him to his desk for at least a week. It was her way of keeping him out of trouble, and he knew it but didn't complain. The truth was, Navid knew how much Duncan had wanted to see him, see the look on his face when he was released, to rub his nose in it. To ignore him was to punish him and as much as it pissed him off, Navid knew it might be the closest thing he'd get to justice. It wasn't nearly enough but it was all he could do, until he caught him in the act again, that is.

He kept his ear to the ground but his informants had all stopped taking his calls. He couldn't blame them. He'd gotten one of them killed and in certain circles, news like that traveled fast. He'd be lucky if any of them ever spoke to him again but he was sure they would not.

Four uneventful days went by and with how quiet it seemed, he was beginning to think Lawrence had been killed. A less likely scenario was that he was keeping his nose clean, or at least pretending he was.

"Parsi," he said, answering the landline on his desk.

"Hey, Navid, it's Charlie." His voice was weak and solemn with a twinge of defeat.

"Charlie, my favorite PO." He leaned back, rolling his eyes, already sure of what he was going to say by the guilty frustration in his tone.

"I just wanted to give you a heads up, Lawrence hasn't checked in."

"You don't say."

"He was on my schedule for Wednesday. It's now Friday and no word."

"Shocking, seriously. I can hardly believe it."

"That's enough sarcasm, Nav. Now, I've already requested a recall but..."

"But, what?"

He was quiet for a time, his silence answer enough.

"Let me guess, you can't find him."

A dejected sigh was his only response.

"That's all right, Charlie. I expected as much." He hung up and made a beeline for Pen's office, barging in and slamming the door.

She shot him an annoyed glance. "I'll call you back," she said, hanging up her phone. "Charlie call you, too?"

"Just now. Can you believe this?"

"Sadly, yes."

"What are we gonna do about it, then?"

"Same as always, track him down, bring him in. He'll get fourteen days and be right back out there. I've got to tell you, Navid, this is getting exhausting."

"That's facts."

"I don't know how much longer I can do this. We put criminals away and the higher-ups let them walk. We haul them back in, they get out, and on and on. I'm sick of it. I've spent fifteen years climbing the ranks and for what? This isn't the first time, you know. At least six times a year some tosser gets let out who has no right to be. Always rich. Always connected. I hate to say it but the system is fucked."

He planted his hands on her desk and leaned in, eyes focused on hers and expression determined. "Then, let's unfuck it."

She bit her bottom lip, her pupils dilating and her pale cheeks flushing. She nodded, blowing out a breath. "Let's."

"We start with Lawrence. We've had his warehouse staked for a while now and no one's come to move those crates of stolen goods. They'll have to at some point, yeah?"

She nodded again, staring up at him through blond lashes.

"We put the screws to him, threaten him, whatever we've got to do to get him to talk, tell us who he's been payin' off and for how long. If he won't spill, we'll investigate everyone, in secret. Bobbies, judges, whoever. I'll take on the whole department, I don't give a--'

"I'm with you," she said, getting to her feet. "Whatever it takes."

Navid got home late, leaving his phone and gun on the bar and sitting on the sofa, worn out from endless paperwork and aggravating conversations. The flat was dark save for the kitchen light that cast an eerie yellow glow throughout the living area. He wondered how many more quiet nights like this he'd get. With the baby coming, he was sure his alone time was soon to come to an end. That was fine. He was looking forward to it, the feedings and the snuggles. The diapers not so much but even that didn't concern him. He was excited to become a father, one his son could be proud of.

He lifted the remote to watch a little TV before heading to bed but was stopped by a familiar voice from behind. "I wouldn't do that if I was you," the man said.

He dropped the remote and stood, whipping around to see Duncan Lawrence standing in the hall, blocking the path between him and the bedrooms. Rage boiled over as he asked through gritted teeth, "Where's Phindi?"

"Your wife?" Duncan asked, pointing his thumb to the bedroom door. "Pretty thing, she is. Getting big, isn't she? Now, why didn't you mention you had a little one comin'? I would've sent a gift."

He edged toward the bar, one tiny step at a time. "Breakin' in my place, that's brave of ya. You want to be arrested?"

"We both know that's not gonna happen, don't we?"

"You're right. I don't have to arrest you. You broke in here, obviously tryin' to come off threatenin'. It'd be in my rights to kill you right here. No jury in the world would convict me. I'd be justified."

He chortled. "You ain't gonna kill me, Parsi. You're too much of a stand-up guy. Noble, you are. It's a shame, too 'cause once I'm done with ya, I'm gonna pay your blond friend a visit. You know the one. Blue eyes, button nose. Your boss."

"Pen? Good luck. She'll see you comin' from miles away. You think I'm a pain in your ass? Give her an excuse and she'll be your worst nightmare. She'll have you on your knees and in cuffs before you can say plea bargain."

"Oh, I'm not gonna hurt her. I'm gonna recruit her. Offer her somethin' she can't get workin' straight."

"Money?" He laughed. "She's fine on that front, bruv. 'Sides, she's good at her job. Better than me. Better than anyone. You can't corrupt her."

"Maybe you're right. Who knows? Who cares? If she won't play ball, I'll off her and replace her with someone who will. There's no shortage of underpaid scuffers willing to look the other way for a little financial security. Uh, uh." He wagged his finger as Navid got closer to the bar. "I see what you're doin', Nav. Not very sportsman-like."

He stopped, his heart in his stomach as he asked the question, "What did you do to Phindi?"

"Nothin', Jesus. The bird's with child, isn't she? I'm a criminal, Parsi, not a monster."

"Yeah, well, forgive me if I don't take you at your word."

"It's a shame she'll have to find you, though, all covered in blood with a hole through ya. Might be such a shock she goes into labor a bit early. She's close enough, though, right? The kid would be all right."

"I swear to fuckin' God--"

"Shouldn't do that, mate. He's always watchin'."

"In fact, he's not." He made note of the pistol on Duncan's hip, the dim lighting hiding it in shadow until now. "He's takin' a rest." He dove to the bar, reaching for his weapon. Duncan drew, pointing his gun at Navid. The detective got two shots off, one bullet hitting the wall next to Duncan's arm and the other flying into his left thigh.

"Fuck!" Lawrence shouted, dropping to the floor.

"Drop it, Lawrence," he said, moving closer, gun pointing at the criminal's chest.

"So you can arrest me?" He panted, obviously trying to feign strength in the face of immense pain, blood gushing from his blown-out femoral artery.

"That's right."

"Not bloody likely, mate."

They were in a standoff, weapons locked on each other, neither willing to accept defeat.

"What is that racket?" Phindi called from down the hall. Navid looked up, taking his eyes off Lawrence to see his wife opening the bedroom door.

"Stay there!" he called.

He'd only looked away for a second. Just long enough to see his wife's location, to make sure she wasn't in the path of his bullet should he have to shoot again. But, a second was all it took. Duncan fired his weapon, two bullets hitting Navid directly in the chest.

"Navid!" he heard his wife shout. As his knees hit the floor, his vision going blurry, he watched her race up the hall. The last thing he saw before the world went black was her grabbing Duncan's head, jerking it to the right, and snapping his neck.

Doctors worked for hours removing the bullets, Navid in and out of consciousness, unable to feel his body. Once in a while, he could hear Phindi somewhere in the distance yelling at someone, demanding she be allowed to see him. That it was her right. Beeps and muffled voices surrounded him with the occasional flash of bright light breaking through the darkness behind his eyes. He thought he should be sleeping. If he was in the hospital, presumably they were operating on him and if that were so, he should be sleeping under anesthesia. So, why wasn't he? Why was he nothing but a stream of endless thoughts trapped in his body? And, then it occurred to him. He wasn't sleeping because he wasn't on his way to getting better. He was dying.

The noises of the hospital began to move farther and farther away as if he were being pulled down an invisible corridor. Darkness enfolded him, black the only thing he could see. Even his own thoughts faded as his monitor flat-lined, its high-pitched drone mixing with Phindi's far-off scream. A moment later, there was nothing. No noise, no thoughts, no worries. There was just...nothing.

Chapter 5

NAVID WOKE UP FREEZING under a sheet in the hospital's morgue, lying on a metal table and covered in goosebumps. He sat up, his hand flying to his chest. He looked down at his healed flesh, rubbing the spot where he'd been fatally wounded, no evidence of his injuries remaining save the dull ache that lingered in and around his heart. Had it been a dream? It couldn't have been. If he'd just been asleep, he wouldn't have woken up naked in the basement with a sheet over his head. There was only one explanation. "Gabriel," he whispered, expecting to see the snarky angel pop out from behind something with a quip about how long it took to bring him back. "Gabriel, are you here?" No answer came. She must have healed him and taken off. She was busy, he knew. She probably did her thing and left in a hurry. He blew out a relieved breath, hopping off the table and wrapping the sheet around his waist. His clothes were nowhere to be found, probably in a bag. Probably with Phindi. "Awe, Phin," he muttered to himself. She'd seen him get shot, witnessed him die. *She must be a wreck,* he thought, stepping gingerly to the door and peeking out. The clock on the wall was set to four-thirty-seven and by what he could see of the sky through the hopper window at the end of the hall, it was AM meaning he'd been "dead" for at least four hours, probably more. He had to get out of there, and get home. He didn't want Phindi grieving for a second longer than she had to. So, draped in a sheet and with bare feet he slipped into the hall and then into the stairwell where he climbed up to the first floor. From there, he was able to sleuth unnoticed out an exit and into the car park. It was only a few blocks to his flat so he decided to walk, not that he had a choice at this hour with no phone. Hopefully, on his way, he wouldn't get nicked for indecent exposure.

The pavement was cool and wet under his feet as he made his way home, a light drizzle chilling his exposed skin. He kept to the shadows as best he could, not wanting to draw attention to himself. Luckily for him, no one was out but a delivery driver and the baker he was delivering to and neither of them took notice as they were engaged in a heated argument about the rising cost of baguettes. Finally, he was at his building, warm in the elevator, his shoulders relaxing as the lift's doors closed him in.

In the hall, he knocked on his own door. With no keys to get in, he hoped the middle-of-the-night tapping wouldn't frighten his wife too terribly. She should be asleep but he was sure she wouldn't be. Not with everything that had happened. Gabriel must have told her what she'd done. Phindi was probably inside, waiting for him to come home, ready to give him another speech about the dangers of his work. Standing there, ache in his chest and fresh from the morgue, he could see she had a point.

The door flew open, his own gun pointed at his head. "It's me!" he said, holding one hand in front of him as if to say "Stop".

"Navid?" Phindi said through buckets of tears. "How?"

"Gabriel, I think," he said, surprised but not shocked that the angel hadn't filled her in. "You want to let me in or do you like holdin' me at gunpoint?"

"Navid," She tossed the gun to the ground and pulled him inside, throwing her arms around him and kissing his cheek four times.

He kicked the door closed and held her close, careful not to squeeze too hard. "I'm all right. I'm not a hundred percent sure how but I am."

"I don't care how you are with me. All that matters is that you are."

He pulled back and wiped the tears from her eyes. "No more cryin' for me, yeah? I'm fine."

She nodded, drying her cheeks with the sleeve of her nightgown. "Even your old bruises are gone."

"That's the power of angels, innit? Is there anything to eat? I feel like I haven't eaten in weeks."

She ignored him, whipping the sheet away and getting to her knees.

"I appreciate the thought, love, but you don't have to--" He gasped as she took him into her mouth. He braced himself against the door as she went to work, his knees going weak. "But, if you insist."

They slept until early afternoon, ordering a huge lunch and watching a movie. They ate and relaxed, enjoying their time together after such a terrifying ordeal the night before. When Phindi dozed off on the couch, he sent flowers via a website on his phone to Gabriel with a note that read, *Thanks for bringing me back*, knowing that if he called and gushed, it would only make her uncomfortable. She was trying to live as normally as she could since God left her in New York and she hated when he treated her like the angel she was. Flowers would show his gratitude without making her feel like he was worshiping her.

It had only been a couple of hours since the last time he'd eaten but he was starving, rifling through the pantry for any snack he could find. He inhaled a full bag of crisps and half a box of biscuits before finishing off the leftover pizza in the fridge.

"What are you doing?" Phindi asked, rubbing her eyes as she met him in the kitchen.

"Nothin', just hungry. Comin' back from the dead burns a lot of calories, apparently."

She studied his face. "You're not a zombie, are you? I've heard stories."

He blinked. "I--I don't think so."

She got closer, inspecting his eyes. "No, you are fine."

"How do you know?"

"Your cornea's are not clouded, no Tache noir or Kevorkian sign. You are truly alive, not a simple reanimated corpse."

"Well, that's good to know, innit?"

"Yes." She gave him a peck on the lips. "Very good. You should thank the Messenger for what she's done."

"Already handled it. Sent her some sunflowers. The website said they mean gratitude. And, I've been thinkin' about it and maybe you're right."

"Of course I am. About what?"

"My work. Maybe--'

"You will quit?!" She beamed, her face lighting up as she nearly hopped with excitement.

"*Maybe, after* I clean up some of the corruption in this town, I will *consider* retiring."

"Maybe is a start." She kissed him again, her hand on his cheek.

He should retire. It was clear as day after what had happened. Gabriel wouldn't always be there to pull him back from the brink. In fact, the night he died was the first time in over a year since he'd been in the same country as her. Thanks to his wife, Duncan Lawrence was off the map and no longer a threat but there were others, dozens, maybe hundreds of criminals he'd locked up that would love nothing more than to come for revenge. And, maybe they would get their chance if he and Pen couldn't bring down the dirty cops and paid-off judges. This thing could go all the way up to politicians. It would be a surprise to no one if it did. It could take months, years even to catch everyone involved, if it was possible at all which was why he emphasized the word "maybe". He didn't want to promise Phindi something he couldn't deliver. Still, he'd put her through enough. He knew that when the baby came, she'd force him to make a decision: his work, or his family.

Chapter 6

W HEN MONDAY CAME, NAVID went back to work. Armed with a story about a bulletproof vest, he hoped no one would question how he'd made it out of the hospital alive. They did, of course, but the lie seemed to be believed. With him there, walking around and breathing, what choice did they have but to buy his story? Now, all he had to do was convince Pen to put him back in the field. Lawrence was dead but his operations were still running, not to mention the systemic corruption in the city's justice system. He had work to do and dying a little wasn't going to stop him from getting it done.

"Parsi," Pen called from the door to her office.

He sighed, knowing he was in for yet another lecture. He followed her inside, ready to defend his decision to come back to work so soon after the incident. But, after closing the door and the blinds, she threw her arms around his neck, squeezing him tightly for a solid ten seconds.

"We were told you were gone," she said, her voice muffled in his shoulder as the collar of his white button-down grew damp with her tears.

He rubbed her back and gave it a pat. "They must've confused me with someone else." He pulled away to look her in the eye. "I'm fine. See?" He did a slow twirl, offering a gentle smile. "Not a scratch on me."

She nodded, wiping the mascara streaks from her cheeks and chin. "You gave us all quite a fright." She pulled a tissue from its box on her desk, tapped it to her tongue, and used it to clean the mess she'd made on his shirt. "We were plannin' a memorial."

"I should've waited to come back, then," he joked. "I would've liked to hear what people 'round here *really* think of me."

"The word tossed around most was, 'intense'."

He pressed his tongue to his cheek. "I can see that."

"I want you here for a while, at your desk."

"Pen,"

"You can research crooked cops and corrupt judges from a computer here as well as anywhere else."

"Sure, but what about the Mares?"

"Duncan's dead, thanks to your wife. You know, I didn't think she had it in her, snappin' his neck and that. She seems so domestic."

He stifled a laugh, his memory of her as a fierce vampire army general not exactly something he could share. "You don't know her that well."

"I guess not."

"So the warehouse,"

"No." She walked around her desk and sat, using her computer's black screen as a mirror as she did what she could to fix her eye makeup.

"Word 'round the office is they're bustin' a big buy tonight."

"I said no, Navid. I don't want to put you in any more danger for the time bein'."

"Come on, Pen. I'll wear a vest. I'll take every precaution."

"Every precaution is plantin' your ass right here."

"It's somethin' I've got to tidy up, yeah? Them Mare Boys have been a thorn in my side for years. I'll wrap them up then I swear, I'll stay put."

She scoffed.

"I'm serious, Pen. It's eatin' at my brain like an unfinished task. I have to bust these guys. Then, I'll work solely on the corruption stuff, I promise."

She arched a brow. "Solely?"

"Yeah, well, the Mrs. wants me to..." He paused, not sure if he could say it out loud.

"She, wants you to what?"

"Retire."

She burst out laughing, smacking the desk with the palm of her hand. "Retire? *You?*"

"Yeah, well, with the baby comin',"

"No, I get it, it's just...I mean, you know how you are."

"I do." He sat across from her, shoulders slumped. "I don't know if I can do it, Pen. I should, I know that. It just feels like this is what I'm supposed to do, fightin' injustice, locking criminals away. I want to do right by her, by my family but..."

"Just like me, you are. My dad was a cop, his dad was a cop. It's in our blood."

He thought about his dad, Allydia, and Cain and shook his head. "Not exactly. The opposite, I think."

"Whatever, I'm not letting you go on that raid."

"Please, Pen. I have to clean this up. I'll do anything. I'll clean the bloody toilets if that's what it takes."

"For Christ's sake, fine. But, I'm leadin'. You stay close and don't make a move without my say-so, you got it?"

"Yeah," He stood, a twinkle in his chestnut eyes. "Whatever you say." He hurried back to his desk, not wanting to give her the chance to change her mind.

His phone buzzed in his pocket. Gabriel was calling him. "Hey," he answered.

"Got your flowers," she said as he sat in his office chair.

"Ah, good. Thanks again."

"Yeah, see, I have no idea what you're thanking me for. The card said I brought you back. The fuck are you talking about?"

"You know," He glanced around, lowering his voice so as not to be heard by anyone but the angel. "Bringing me *back.*"

"Back from what? Are you high?"

"The other night. The hospital. None of this ringin' a bell?"

"Bro, I haven't been in a hospital in years. I don't get sick."

"But," His stomach dropped, his chest tightening.

"But, what?"

"Gabriel, can I ask, where were you Friday night?"

"Here, at home. What's going on with you?"

"I--I don't--"

"Dude, you're spiraling."

He swallowed the lump in his throat. *The time difference*, he thought. *That has to explain it. It was day to her. Maybe.* "Gabriel, when was the last time you were in London?"

"Your wedding three years ago. What's your deal, bro? You on a bender? Sleeping okay? Drinking enough water?"

"I..." He fell back in his seat, his mind racing and his limbs going numb. "I've got no idea." He ended the call and set the phone on the desk, letting his hands fall to his lap and whispering to himself, "What the fuck?"

That night, just after sundown, Navid followed Pen and a handful of bobbies to the Mare's storage warehouse. There, they spotted seven men, all armed, some with guns, some with Bowie knives. They were loading crates onto a semi, the driver barking at them to hurry.

"Everybody, freeze!" Pen said, weapon drawn.

"Pigs!" someone shouted.

"Aw, fuck this," the driver said, pulling away, leaving most of his cargo on the floor and the back of his truck still up.

What was left of the Mare's went into a frenzy, opening fire on the bobbies, taking out most of them with little effort.

"Should've been armed with somemthin' other than fuckin' tasers," Navid grumbled as he took aim at a man running toward him. He took a shot, blowing out his kneecap and sending him falling to the ground with a thud.

"Not my call," Pen defended, shooting another criminal in the back as he attempted to flee.

Bullets whizzed by as Navid tried to find cover so he could reload while Pen took out two more men. He made it to a stack of crates and pulled out his empty clip but before he could replace it with a new one he felt a sudden sting followed by a sharp ache in the side of his neck. His hands turned to ice as blood poured down his shirt and he dropped to his knees.

"Navid!" Pen screamed, emptying her clip into the man standing over him, the gangster's knife clattering on the cement next to him as he fell. With everyone else dead or in the wind, she holstered her weapon and rushed to kneel in front of him, Navid falling forward into her.

She rested his head in her lap and gently slapped his cheek. "Navid, can you hear me?"

"Y--yes," he gurgled, his eyes wide.

"I'm calling an ambulance, all right? Just stay with me."

"No," he begged. "No hospital."

"Are you daft?" She took her Tetra from her belt. "Your carotid's been nicked. You're bleedin' out."

"Please," He fought to explain, knowing full well an ambulance would never make it in time. "Just get me somewhere private."

"You don't know what you're sayin'."

Sparks closed in around his vision as the light in the room seemed to fade. With his last bit of energy, he told her, "I wasn't wearin' a vest, Pen."

"What are you on about?"

"The other night. I wasn't--" His eyes fluttered closed.

"Navid," She slapped his cheek again. "Navid!"

"I think...I'm sure," He opened his eyes just a little, his vision gone but his ears still working. "I'll be right back."

Chapter 7

NAVID WOKE WITH A start, his hand flying to his neck, a hint of pain still lingering. Garbage bags rustled underneath him as he looked around to see where he was. He recognized the lilac-painted walls straight away. He was at Pen's.

He sat up to see her there, trembling on the sofa a few feet away. "Platic bags were smart," he told her. "Protected the carpet from," He pointed at his now healed neck. "You know."

"You were dead," she said, her voice little more than a whisper. Her cheeks were streaked with mascara-laced tears and her clothes were stained with his blood. Eyes puffy and cheeks red, he could see how upset she'd been. "I watched you die. I held you in my arms and I cried. I pleaded with whatever deity would listen for it not to be true. I could feel my heart breakin'. I sat in that warehouse for an hour begging you to wake up."

His tone softened. "Pen,"

"After a while, I gave up. I had to accept it. I was about to call it in when I saw your wound," She paused, shaking her head like she still couldn't believe it. "I saw it close up. Fixed, on its own. Color started comin' back to your face. I felt for your pulse and there it was, weak, slow, but there. I didn't know what to do so I stuffed you in the boot of my car and brought you back here where I've sat, just like this for the last three hours."

"I'm so sorry you had to see that but--"

She held her hand up to stop him, unable to hide how much she was still shaking. "I just have one question."

He nodded for her to go ahead.

"What the fuck are you?"

"What do you--"

"You're not human, right? People don't just spontaneously come back to life. So, what are you? Alien? Werewolf? Vampire?"

"Vampires don't actually exist anymore."

"Anymore?"

"I'm human, Pen, I just...I can't explain it. I think it must be a genetic thing."

"A genetic thing? This isn't red hair or freckles, Navid. *You came back to life.*"

"Some of my ancestors could, too. It's complicated but I think I inherited somethin'. Some latent Lazarus-type gene or--"

"What the fuck, Navid?!"

"I don't know!" he shot back, getting to his feet, his legs wobbly. "I don't know what's goin' on with me and that's the truth." He sat next to her, begging with his eyes. "You're not gonna tell anyone about this, are ya, Pen?"

She blew out a steadying breath, her expression telling him she wasn't sure.

"Please, Pen. I've got a son comin'. If people find out about my...*condition* they'll lock me away, run experiments. I've got to be there for my family. Please."

She looked him over, fresh tears welling in her bloodshot eyes. "You seem like yourself."

"I am. I'm no different than I ever was just now I'm..."

"Immortal?"

"I honestly don't know."

She blew out another breath, her sharp features relaxing. "All right, I'll keep this between us *for now* but I don't want to see you back at work for a while."

"What do you mean?"

"I'm serious. You've got to take a leave of absence or a vacation or something, at least until you figure out what's going on."

"You're bein' a tad unreasonable, Pen."

"I just watched you *die*, dragged your ass back here, my back still hurts, by the way, and then saw you wake up like you'd just been takin' a nap."

He sighed.

"What if someone else had seen that? Seen you on the ground, all corpse-like? If anyone else had been there you would've woken up in the morgue."

"Again," he mumbled.

"Jesus Christ."

"It was just the once."

"It's only because I care about you that I'm not reporting this, this, whatever the fuck this is. But, I swear to God, if you sprout fangs or a tail or somethin', I'm choppin' your bloody head of myself."

"Very nice, Pen."

"If you'd seen what I'd seen--"

"No, I get it. I understand. But, I promise, I'm not a monster. I'm just me but..."

"Also, somethin' else."

He shook his head. "I'll figure it out. I swear."

"Good, because I don't want to have to kill you, permanently this time."

He chuckled.

"Give me your shirt."

"What?"

"It's covered in blood. You can't walk 'round the city lookin' like that. One of your old ones is still in my closet somewhere. I'll fetch it for you and wash this one."

His brows furrowed in confusion. "You held on to one of my shirts?"

"Well," she defended. "You wouldn't talk to me for months so I couldn't exactly bring it by your flat and after a while, I forgot it was there. By the time I remembered, it had been so long and we were finally gettin' on again. I didn't want to bring up bad memories."

"Yeah, I get that."

"Off with it, then. I'll soak it in some peroxide. Should lift right out."

"All right," He stood, unbuttoned his shirt, and slid out of it. He handed it to her as she, too got to her feet. His skin prickled, his sleeveless undershirt providing no warmth in her cool apartment. "Thanks, Pen."

"Don't mention it. Seriously, ever."

He nodded, a weak smile on his lips. She moved past him, heading to the kitchen where she placed the stained shirt in the sink and got a bottle of peroxide from the cabinet. Lightheaded, he sat back down, his stomach grumbling. "Hey, Pen,"

"Yeah?"

"You got any snacks?"

Walking home, the ache in his neck fading and his hunger not yet satiated, he decided not to tell Phindi about what had happened that night. It would only worry her and since he had no real idea why or how this was happening, he wouldn't be able to calm her nerves about it. She needed rest and a stress-free environment, and he would give it to her as best he could.

In the stillness of the late spring night, he tried to make sense of it. Maybe it *was* a genetic thing. Cain had been immortal. It had taken the actual Wrath of God to put an end to him. Allydia had been immortal until a witch eradicated vampirism. But his mother was killed, snuffed out by his evil ancestor. Maybe it skipped a generation...or a thousand.

He got home to Phindi napping on the sofa, dinner in a pot on the stove, the burner set to low to keep it warm. He knelt in front of her and lightly stroked her cheek, marveling at her beauty as he woke her. "Phin," He kissed her forehead. "Phin, love, do want dinner or should I let you sleep?"

"Navid," she said, opening her eyes and stretching her legs. "You're late."

"Yeah, sorry. We were bustin' the last of the Mare Boys. Only two got away and they were low on the roster. Shouldn't be a problem from here on out."

"That's good."

"And, I have another bit of news I think you'll like."

She sat up and he took a set next to her. "What is it?"

"I'm takin' a leave of absence. Not sure for how long but--"

"What did you do?" she asked, her tone accusatory.

He blinked. "What do you mean?"

"You wouldn't do that voluntarily so I am guessing you did something reckless...again."

He didn't want to lie but he couldn't tell her the truth, at least not the *whole* truth. Not without stressing her out so he chose his words carefully. "I didn't do anything, Pen just thinks I should take some time."

She rolled her eyes. "Oh, of course. Penelope told you to do something so you listen but when I beg you for months to do the same thing it's 'Oh, I don't know, maybe'."

"All right, first, you want me to quit, not just take a break and secondly, there's no arguin' with Pen. She's my boss."

"Pfft, *boss*."

"She is."

"Yes, but that is irrelevant."

"You lost me."

"She would like that, wouldn't she?"

"I'm tryin' to follow, love but you've got to give me a hint."

She stood. "She still has feelings for you, I can tell. Romantic feelings."

He got up to look her in the eye. "She doesn't."

"Do you think I haven't seen the way she looks at you? I have. Like a dog with a steak. She knows it is not for her but she wants it, anyway."

"Phin, she has no interest in me. Even if she did, it makes no difference. I love *you*. Only you."

"I know that." She gave him a peck on the cheek. "And, I am happy you'll be home and out of danger. I just wish you could see what I see."

"I really don't think she still has a thing for me," he said, even as he began to question it in his mind. The way she reacted to his deaths, saying her heart broke when she thought he was gone...the shirt. Maybe she *was* still carrying a torch for him. Poor thing.

"She does. Trust me, a woman's instincts are never wrong."

"So, what you're sayin' is, you won the prize." He flashed a toothy grin, hoping to lighten the mood.

She laughed. "I did, yes. Just don't forget that you were very lucky, as well."

"I never will." He kissed her gently then made his way to the kitchen. "You sit back down. I'll get dinner ready."

She let out a relieved sigh as she sat. "Thank you, mpenzi."

"You're welcome, darling." As he gathered bowls and spoons, his stomach growling and his mouth watering, he considered what she'd said. He wasn't sure one way or the other but what he'd told her was true. Pen could feel however she liked. He was happy with Phindi. Still, he didn't want things to be awkward between him and Pen. Maybe this leave of absence was just what they all needed. He was safe, enjoying his time with his wife and preparing for the arrival of their son and Pen would have the distance she needed to move on, if, that is, she hadn't already.

Chapter 8

I T HAD BEEN TWO hours since Phindi went to sleep but Navid was restless. He stayed up in bed, reading Lailani Wright and snacking on his favorite crisps. He shifted to a more comfortable position, his legs tingling with pins and needles. He read another chapter, the twinges getting stronger, distracting him from the story. He looked at the time and decided his body was telling him he needed sleep, even if he didn't feel tired. He put his tablet on the nightstand and took a drink of water, swinging his legs over the side of the bed. But, before he could get up to brush his teeth, sharp pains zinged up his calves and thighs causing the muscles to twitch. He winced, staying quiet to not wake his wife. He rubbed his legs, stretching them out in front of him and kicking the air in an attempt to get the circulation going. It didn't help.

Within seconds, the pain spread up to his abdomen, like muscle cramps mixed with stabbing pain, sharp and radiating. He doubled over with a wave of nausea, stumbling out of bed and to the bathroom where he threw up in the sink, unable to keep the acid in his throat down long enough to get to the toilet. He rinsed his mess down the drain and swished out his mouth but as the nausea dissipated, the pain grew worse, rising through his abdomen to his chest, burning like lava filling his veins. An invisible force gripped his heart like a vise, his breath catching in his throat as vertigo knocked him to his knees. Was he having a heart attack? Would he die again and if he did, would he come back this time?

Struggling to breathe, he began to cough, blood spraying onto the bathroom tile. He clutched his chest, fighting for air, his vision once again going blurry. Flopping to his side, he hoped he would again be resurrected and before Phindi woke up. But, as the world went dim, he could hear her calling for him. Soon, she was standing over him, wide-eyed and crestfallen.

She knelt to touch his cheek, her eyes beginning to pool. The last thing he heard before he died was her quiet voice saying, "It can not be."

The bright bathroom light burned his eyes as they blinked open, Phindi's voice over him as she talked to someone on the phone. "He is awake," she said. "Yes, seven minutes." She handed him the phone as he sat up, his head pounding and his heart aching. He felt weak, exhausted, and starving. "It is the queen."

He held the cell to his ear and cleared his throat. "Hey, Gran."

"You should have called me sooner," Allydia lectured.

"Good to hear from you as always."

"Don't be smart. This is no time for sarcasm. You have to leave. *Now.*"

"What?"

"Phindi has packed you a bag. There will be a jet waiting for you at Heathrow."

"What are you on about, Gran? What do you mean, leave?"

"The country."

"*The country?*"

"It's the only way to prevent this from happening again. At least, for a while. The plane will take you to Edinburgh where you can stay with your father."

"My, father? You know I can't stand him. Why would I--"

"I know he is a bit unsavory but he did say you could visit any time and right now you need to be somewhere else."

"I really don't see why--'

"Go this instant! I'll send help." She ended the call, Navid staring down at the phone in confusion. He looked down at himself, realizing he was out of his pajamas and in a pair of jeans and a tee shirt, socks, and shoes that had been in the other room now on his feet. 'How the..."

"I dressed you," Phindi told him, shoving a duffel bag in his hands. "There is very little time." She took him by the arm and walked him to the front door.

"Wait, wait," he protested. "I don't know what you and Gran think is going on here but I'm not going anywhere. Not without you."

"I shouldn't fly and you have no time to waste." She pushed him out the door. "Please go. I can not bear to watch you die again." She closed the door in his face and he stood in the hall, bewildered, his legs like jelly. He heard the locks click and the chain slide into place. He couldn't get back in now unless he broke the door down and he didn't have the strength for that. So, as much as it confused and irritated him, he got in the elevator, thinking to himself, *I guess I'm going to see my dad.*

Once on the plane, the lingering aches and pains had begun to fade. Once in the air, they were all but gone. Still tired and hungry, he shoveled crisps and biscuits in his mouth by the fistful, washing them down with two tins of water. When the rumbling in his stomach had quieted, he leaned his head back and closed his eyes, getting a nap in before landing in Scotland.

By the time he got to Giovanni's flat, the sun had begun to rise. It was far too early to knock, six in the morning hardly an appropriate time for a surprise visit. Coupled with the fact that he hadn't seen his father since the wedding three years before, he wasn't sure how he'd be received. Should he use the key he'd been given for emergencies? Or should he go somewhere for breakfast and come back in a few hours? As he contemplated his options, the door flew open, Giovanni jumping at the sight of him.

"Navid, my boy!" he said, taking his face in his hands and kissing his cheeks. "Was I expecting you?"

"No. Is it a bad time? I can come back.'

"Don't be silly! You are always welcome here. Sadly, I can not stay." He picked up two suitcases and scooted past him into the hall. "I have to go to Italy for a little while. Would you like to come with me? I could show you where we come from, introduce you to our cousins. Get you some real Italian food, eh? Fatten you up a little?" He pat his abs. "You look thin. Is your wife feeding you properly? That reminds me, I've been meaning to send you my Nonna's recipes. That woman made the most beautiful cacio e pepe you've ever tasted. On my life, the best cook in all of Italy."

Mildly relieved he wouldn't have to spend much time with him, he shook his head. "Thank you but no. I just need a place to stay for a few days while I'm in town. I can go to a hotel."

"Don't be ridiculous. You can stay here. My home is your home. You still have a key, yes?"

He pat his jean's pocket, grateful Phindi had thought to put them there while he was a corpse. "Yes."

"Then it's settled. If I'm not back by the time you leave, give me a call. We'll catch up." He pat his shoulder. "Oh, and if anyone comes looking for me, just tell them you don't know when I'll be back."

"I *don't* know when you'll be back."

"So, it's not a lie." He lightly tapped his cheek and gave him a smile, walking to the elevator and closing himself in.

Navid waited until he was gone to go inside, locking the door behind him and dropping his bag on the coffee table. He sank into the couch, wondering which he should do first, eat or sleep. But, his exhaustion made the decision for him, his eyes closing and mind going blank as much-needed sleep overtook him.

Chapter 9

H E AWOKE TO POUNDING on the door as loud as the pounding in his head, wiping the sleep from his eyes and cracking his neck. He stood, stretching his legs and arms as he made his way to the door. When he opened it, he was surprised to see who was standing there, arms crossed over her band tee shirt and her features scrunched.

"Gabriel? What are you doin' here?"

"Why didn't you call me?" she asked, pushing her way in and dropping her bag on the coffee table next to his.

He closed the door, fighting back a yawn. "Seemed like a family matter."

"I'm not family? My brother's married to your ancestor."

"Forgive me but I don't generally think 'family' when I think of someone I've seen half-naked."

"Lucky you. Speaking of half-naked, my tits *have* held up well, thanks for noticing. Try to stop thinking about them now, though. It's kind of creepy."

"I wasn't," He stopped, remembering who he was talking to. "I'm sorry."

"It's cool. Hypersexuality runs in your genes."

"It does?"

"Like a cheetah." She moved closer, her stare so intense he needed to take a step back. "Oh, yeah, that Pen girl is desperate for that D. Pretend you don't know, it'll be less awkward." She took her phone from her back pocket and began typing.

"What are you doing?"

"Texting Phindi."

"What for?"

"Letting her know she's not crazy, that girl is definitely still into you, and that you have zero interest."

"Why would you--"

"It's the right thing to do. Anyway, let me look at you." She put her phone on the table and stared again, this time for an uncomfortable amount of time. "Yep, that's what I thought."

"What?"

"You got Cain's curse. You remember that weird envelope of blood and hair you got a few years ago?"

He thought for a few seconds then it came to him. "The one with the dead leaves?"

"Herbs, yeah. It was a spell transferring his curse to you." She looked annoyed. "This has Lilith written all over it."

"Lilith? But, how--"

"It got triggered when you died. I have no idea how she pulled it off. Also," She smacked his arm.

"Ow," he winced, rubbing the spot, suddenly remembering how strong she was.

"Be more careful. If you die for real before Dia, she'll fall the fuck apart and if she's depressed near me, I'll be depressed and you know I don't have time for that shit right now."

"Well, I wouldn't want to be a burden."

"You say that with sarcasm but I know you mean it." She sighed, folding her arms again. "You're not a burden, Navid. More like...an unfinished task."

Another round of knocking came on the door.

"Uh, oh."

"What?"

"Cops," she told him, opening his backpack. "Here for your dad."

He rolled his eyes, walking back to open the door and muttering under his breath, "What's he done this time?"

Two officers stood in the hall, their pasty faces twisted in scowls. "Giovanni LaRosa?" the one to the left asked.

"No."

"A client, then?"

"A what?" He couldn't help but be offended by the accusation. He knew what his father did for a living and it turned his stomach. It was one of the many reasons he didn't want to visit let alone be associated with the man.

Gabriel took Navid's wallet from his bag and flashed his warrant card. The officer to the right raised a brow while the other one looked flustered. She handed the wallet to Navid and addressed the Scottish policemen with a fake accent, her tone authoritative. "He's a person of interest in an investigation we're running out of London. I'd ask if you had any information on his whereabouts but since you're here, I'm guessing you're as clueless as we are."

"I guess we are." He handed her a card. "If you find him, let us know. He's suspected of running a brothel."

"I thought prostitution was legal here."

"Sex work, yes," Navid interjected. "Pimping, no. He's taking advantage of these girls, taking a cut of their money. It's not right."

"Exactly," the officer on the right said. "We have witnesses that say he takes half. That's downright greedy."

"If you find him, give us a call," the other cop said, tipping his hat.

"Will do," Navid said, waving goodbye and closing the door. He turned to face the angel. "Quick thinkin'"

"It's easy when you're involuntarily in everyone's head."

"Your accent was terrible by the way."

She shrugged. "Fooled them." She went to the kitchen and rifled through the pantry. "There's nothing to eat here. It's all ingredients. Look at this." She gestured to the cabinet filled with boxes of pasta, various breads, and root vegetables. "What are we supposed to do, starve?"

The rumbling in his stomach had returned. She'd noticed before he did. "We could cook something."

"We could what?" She grimaced. "A, I could never, and two, you haven't cooked for yourself since Phindi got all domestic. Can I just say, what the fuck was that about?"

"What do you mean?"

"She's this badass Zulu warrior, then she's the general of the vampire military, then she opens a gym and teaches self-defense, by the way, not just defense, and then she gets knocked up, and suddenly she's a goddamn housfrau. It's the craziest thing I've ever seen and I've seen some shit."

"She said she wanted--"

"I know, I know. She wants to have a 'normal' life, the life she never thought she'd have. The life her mother wanted for her. Safety, stability, children, picket fences, blah fucking blah. I understand, I just..." She was quiet for a moment as if she were doing math in her head. "Whatever. She's happy so I guess it's fine. Her life." She grabbed a baguette from the cabinet and tossed it to him. "Eat on the way. We have to get to the hospital."

"The hospital? What for? I feel fine now. Just hungry."

"Yeah, that's the curse. The energy it takes to come back from the dead is crazy pants. You'll feel better the longer you go between deaths. The hospital isn't for you."

His brows lifted in confusion. "You all right? I thought you were self-healing."

"I'm fine. Bring your gun."

Walking through the halls of the Old Dalkeith Road hospital, Navid could hold his tongue no longer. "What are we lookin' for, exactly?"

Gabriel scanned doorways and halls, not returning his gaze. "Someone on the verge."

"The verge of what?"

She stopped in front of a room and glanced around. "You see anyone?"

"What?" He looked from one side of the hall to the other. "No, why? What are we doin' here?"

"Shh." She opened the door and dragged him inside before holding a hand over the handle, welding it closed. She then crossed to the bed where a woman of at least seventy lay unconscious, nasal prongs pumping oxygen into her nostrils and a tube down her throat. Gabriel gently removed one of two pillows from under her head and handed it to him.

"What's this?"

"To muffle the noise." The monitor sounded as the old woman flat-lined. "Quick, shoot me."

He blinked. "What?!"

"I need to hitch a ride."

"A ride?"

"To Hell to talk to Lilith. See if there's a way to reverse this curse of yours. Come on, we're on a clock."

"I thought you said humans don't go to Hell?"

"They don't *really* but Purgatory's just a hop, skip, and a jump away. I'll ride the old woman's soul there, find the portal to Hell, pay my unhinged sister a visit, and be back before the doctors know Gerty here has kicked it if you hurry the fuck up and kill me."

"You want me to *kill* you?"

"Just a little bit." She spread her arms wide. "Come on. Right in the heart."

"I don't think I'm comfortable with this."

"Dude, sack up. Pretend I'm a criminal or something."

"I actually try *not* to kill criminals when I shoot at 'em."

"That's super noble of you. You're a regular Boy Scout. Now, *kill me*. I'll be right back, I swear."

"But--"

"Bro, she's almost gone. You can be in your feels about it later."

He blew out a breath and took his weapon from its holster. "I want it on the record I don't want to do this."

"Noted."

He aimed, holding the pillow over the barrel and taking a deep breath.

"Oh, wait." She whipped her shirt off and tossed it on the bed. "Don't want to ruin this top."

He averted his gaze.

"Oh, geez, I have a bra on and it's not like you haven't seen them."

"Just bein' polite."

"Sweet but unnecessary. We both know I'm not shy. Now, shoot me."

He closed his eyes, taking one more deep breath before opening them, again taking aim, and pulling the trigger.

Chapter 10

O UT OF HER BODY, Gabriel floated through Purgatory like a specter, passing yet-redeemed souls in the gray vacuum of Limbo's halls. Lucifer had been right, it *was* grim, hopeless, and devoid of light, emotion, or awareness. Souls hung above, unmoving and unthinking, empty of everything they once were. Like burnt-out light bulbs they dangled in a waiting room for what was to come.

As she searched the ghastly plane, she came upon the souls of James and Esther Murphy, her human parents. Hovering next to each other but unaware of the other's existence, the only things she could feel from them were mourning and regret. "Good," she said, unheard but satisfied.

She continued, eventually reaching the portal, a massive hole poked through the fabric of space and time, blacker than the darkest of nights. She stepped through, mentally preparing herself for what she'd find on the other side.

Her imagination hadn't done the place justice. It was even more decrepit and terrifying than she'd seen in Lucifer's memories. The whole of it was made of onyx and slate, dust as thick and dark as charcoal covering every inch. Even out of her body, she could feel the cold, like death's grip around her being. She tried to sneak through undetected but she shined like a torch in the otherwise dim setting. It was mere seconds before she was spotted, demons in their cages cowering at the sight of her. Screams of "Leave us!" and "What do you want?" erupted from the cells as she passed, getting the attention of the newly minted Watchkeeper of Hell.

"What are you doing here, angel?" he hissed, standing between her and where she needed to be.

"Beelzebub," she said. "Love what you've done with the place."

"This is no place for you."

"So, you're in charge now? I guess someone had to be."

"Why have you come? Is Lucifer to return?"

"Oh, no. That's never happening. I'm just here to have a quick chat with my sister and then I'll be out of your," She looked him over, his black, oval eyes, fly-like wings, and horns the shape of antenna. His feet were hooves at the ends of insect-like legs and his whole body was covered in thin, matted fur. "Hair?" She looked around, the weight of the regrets of the damned like bricks on her heart. "Man, Lucifer's memories didn't do this place justice. It's miserable as fuck."

"It's Hell."

"Yeah, well, it sucks donkey balls. Okay, see you later."

She tried to pass but he grabbed her incandescent arm. "Just a min--"

She threw him back with her mind, sending him reeling into the door of a cell, the occupant scurrying back in fear. "Back the fuck up, Beelz. Out of my body, I'm at full power and I have no kind of time." Fire flashed in her eyes triggering an explosion of screams and shrieks from Hell's inmates. "You don't want to piss me off."

He nodded, avoiding eye contact and keeping out of her way.

She headed down a corridor, her sister's thoughts like a beacon pulling her toward her. At the end of the hall, she found her cell, Lilith inching toward the door.

"Hey, bitch," Gabriel greeted, peering through the bars. She was shocked to see Lilith's tar-like body, a dripping shadow of the girl she'd last possessed. "Keeping it sexy, I see."

"Gabriel? What are you doing here? *Please* tell me Daddy punished you, as well. Oh, it's *delicious*. What did you do? Something violent, I bet. Give me all the details."

"Sorry to disappoint but I'm just here for a chat.'

"Well, that's no fun. I was hoping to torture you a bit."

She ignored her nonsense. "What did you do to Navid?"

"The descendant, yes. Did it work? Is my husband free of Father's curse?"

"He is." Her face was little more than a mass of goop but Gabriel could tell she was pleased. "He's also dead, so..."

"Dead?"

"In Purgatory."

"How?"

"Camael. Stuck him with his plow thing. Anyway, back to Navid."

"Yes, well, that was easy enough. A simple transference spell. I'd tried it a million times but it never worked before. Turns out, all I needed was," She stopped, her thoughts too fast and fractured for Gabriel to make out.

"What?"

She looked at her, bright blue eyes forming on her otherwise pitch-black face. "Samael's blood."

"Samael doesn't have blood."

"He did. When he let me out of here, he put on a body. Just for a few minutes. Just long enough. Wait..."

Their eyes grew wide as they realized at the same time, Gabriel muttering, "Holy shit."

"He was in on it, that bastard!" Lilith screeched so loudly it shook the walls and her cell door. "He was working for Father the entire time! He played me!"

"Fuck me, the puppet-stringing on this guy."

"That's Daddy," she snapped. "Master manipulator."

"I need more answers."

"You said Cain is in Purgatory?"

"Yeah. Oh! That's right! Dead people know everything, even if they're catatonic! Gotta go." She turned to leave.

"Wait, sister!"

She looked over her shoulder. "I'll tell him."

"Thank you."

<hr>

<hr>

Back in Limbo, Gabriel made a mad dash to find Cain, knowing she had little time before her body would be healed and she'd be yanked back into it. Doing her best to ignore the overwhelming nothingness of the souls around her, she reached Cain with minutes to spare. Unlike the other souls there, he looked essentially as he had when he was alive. Instead of hovering in thin air, he sat cross-legged humming to himself. It was strange but since it worked in her favor and she had not a second to spare, she chose to ignore it.

"The angel Gabriel, come to darken further my ever-dark doorstep."

"Lilith says hey."

"Hey?"

She groaned, kneeling in front of him. "She wants you to know she loves you *so much* and she can't wait to see you again."

He sighed. "Even in death, I can not escape her. Although, it might be nice to get to know her without the shackles of our human forms."

"Yeah, she's real handsy. Anyway, I need some information."

"Why should I help you? You had me killed."

"That was not my call and you know it. I actually put it off as long as I could and you were *dying* to die so don't pretend you were inconvenienced somehow. Also, you should be kissing my ass like it's under mistletoe for what I did for Dia."

"Yes, your witch cured her of her affliction, I," he thought for a moment. "Heard?"

"Yeah, it's weird when you just suddenly know something you have no right knowing. I use the term, 'download'."

He chuckled. "I suppose I do owe you a thank you."

"Don't mention it. Anyway, I don't need you to tell me anything. Just be quiet for a sec." She stared into his eyes, rifling through thoughts and memories, peeking at information he came to possess in the years he'd been stuck where he was.

"What do you--"

"Holy shit."

"See something interesting, angel?"

"You could say that." She stood, feeling the pull of her body calling her back. "Okay, well, I'm off. See you in about eight million years."

Chapter 11

G ABRIEL WOKE UP ON the cool tile of the hospital room floor with a gasp, a bullet-holed pillow covering her torso. "God, that fucking sucks."

Navid's muscles relaxed for the first time since he'd shot her. He swallowed the lump in his throat, feeling silly for thinking she might not come back. *She's an angel, moron,* he thought, his nerves calming. "Tell me about it," he replied, offering his hand to help her up and hoping she didn't notice he was slightly trembling. She took it, using the pillow to wipe the blood from her healed chest.

"Really, bro?" She tossed the pillow to the floor and put her top back on.

"For your modesty."

"It's sweet you think I have that." She shoved the pillow in the hazardous waste bin. "Let's get the hell out of here." She giggled to herself. "Hell." She held her hand out, breaking the welded lock.

They slipped out into the hall and hurried to the nearest exit just as a nurse went into the room. Once outside, Navid inquired, "Did you get any answers?"

She pat his shoulder. "Dude, you are gonna shit your pants."

Back at Giovanni's flat, Gabriel sat on the sofa, leaning her head back and closing her eyes. "Man, I am *wiped*. I need a snack. Is there *anything* in that kitchen that doesn't require effort?"

Navid checked the fridge and freezer, finding a pint of chocolate Mackie's. "Ice cream work?"

"Like gangbusters. Gimme." She held her hands out like an impatient child as he opened the carton and took a spoon from a drawer. He gave the items to her and she dug in, her eyes rolling back. "Mm. That's good stuff."

"All right, so spit it out, will ya? What's goin' on?"

"I see you also inherited your ancestor's impatience gene."

"Gabriel,"

"I can't exactly talk about this shit on the tram, can I? Geez." She slapped the cushion next to her. "You're gonna want to sit."

"I take bad news better standin', thanks."

"No, you don't. Why do you think that?"

"Gabriel, I'm beggin' ya, please, get on with it."

She smacked her lips. "*All right.*" She took another bite, flashing a sideways glance. "So, just to ease your mind because I know you've been worrying about it, you didn't do anything to deserve the curse. You're not being punished. It was Cain's curse to bear, you're just carrying it for a little while."

"Sure, yeah, but why?"

She put the carton down on the coffee table and crossed her legs. "So you can break it."

"There's a way?"

"You should really sit."

He cast an aggravated glare.

She threw her hands up. "Have it your way. So, when Cain killed Abel, his girlfriend was pregnant. She--"

"Abel didn't have any kids," he interrupted, his brows scrunched in confusion.

She cocked her head. "You think you know better than me?"

He swallowed hard, mildly terrified of insulting the angel considering what he'd witnessed her do to the mass of vampire corpses in Petra. "I...I'm sorry, it's just, I've read the Koran and the Bible and there's no mention of Abel having children."

"Yeah, well, those books leave out a lot of shit, mess up facts, distort things. Anyways, Abel was supposed to marry Aclima. Cain had a thing for her, too but Abel had already hit that. Part of his jealousy. When Abel died, Aclima was afraid that Cain would either force her to marry him or kill her, too if she refused. So, she took off and Cain married Awan, instead. She got all the way to Armenia before she figured out she was knocked up."

"No offense, but how is this relevant? Why are you tellin' me all this?"

"Context."

He raised a brow.

"Cain wasn't the only one cursed back in the day. Abel's line was marked by his murder. His male descendants are doomed to be killed by their brothers. Not all of them, obvs, but if you're a dude in Abel's line, you have a fifty/fifty chance of ending up on the wrong side of something sharp."

"Right, okay, that sucks for them but what's it got to do with me?"

She took the ice cream from the table and shoved another bite into her mouth, swallowing before answering, "Simple. To break your curse, you have to break theirs."

"How in the hell am I supposed to do that? I'm not a witch or an angel. I'm nothin' but a regular geezer with no special powers to speak of 'cept this comin' back from the dead thing which, if I'm bein' honest, isn't all it's cracked up to be."

She rubbed her chest. "No lies detected."

"Seriously, what am I supposed to do?"

"You have to save the life of one of Abel's descendants thereby mending the cosmic brotherhood or whatever."

"How the hell am I supposed to do that?"

"I don't know, man. *You're* the cop. That's why you got tapped."

"What do you mean?"

"He knew it would be you, my father. The one of your line that's an actual descent person. I mean, don't get me wrong, I love Dia but that bitch is cooky McDoodle face."

"Huh?"

"Crazy. Thousands of years of the most unimaginably fucked up shit you've ever seen. She's all domestic and shit now but deep down she's rowdy as all fuck. Your mom was okay but her dad was a *dick*. My point is, my father chose you to fix this. One of Cain's descendants saving one of Abel's. God's way of righting that original wrong."

"Are you saying," He paused as he tried to wrap his head around what she just told him. "I'm on a mission from God?"

"You're feeling a shaky kind of nauseous combination of honored and horrified?"

"I think I am."

"Been there like, a lot. Welcome to the club." She pat the seat next to her and he finally sat, his knees feeling a little weak.

"Lilith told you all this?"

"Some. The rest I had to dig out of Cain's brain. Not his actual brain, that's dust under the Chelsea. Oh, my God, you should've seen Lilith's face when she found out Cain's curse was lifted. She was so happy, I thought she might cry. That would've been gross, I think, considering the form she's taken."

"Happy? Why would she care? I thought she was evil."

"You know they're a thing, right?"

"Sure, but--"

"My sister is epically fucked in the head but she *does* love him."

"Loves? Present tense? She's dead, yeah?"

"Not *dead* dead. Just in Hell."

"Kind of the definition of bein' dead, innit?"

"I guess from your perspective but death isn't *the end*. More like moving house."

"Right, but you're tellin' me the demon that eats infants and wears little girls like dresses *loves* someone, and from Hell, no less?"

"Peas in a pod, those two. Toxic as all fuck but there's real love there."

"Huh. Well, that's..."

"Fucked up."

"Yeah."

"People complain about me cussing a lot but sometimes there are just no better words to describe things."

He nodded in agreement.

She finished the ice cream and stood. "Okay, I'm gonna go."

"What? *Now?*"

"You know how much shit I have going on right now. I have to get back."

"But--"

"Cain navigated this shit for thousands of years. You can handle it for a few weeks. Just carry some protein bars with you and try not to get offed again."

He stood to face her. "Gabriel, please. I know you're busy but--"

"Bro, this is cop stuff. Track down Abel's descendants. There can't be that many left. Then guard them like a German Shepherd until you arrest or kill their would-be murderer. Detective it up. You got this." She slapped his arm. "I believe in you." She picked up her bag and headed to the door.

"Thanks for your help," he called after her before muttering under his breath. "I guess."

She opened the door. "Welcome."

Chapter 12

P EN ARRIVED THE NEXT day, DNA test kit in hand and attitude in her voice. "You could've ordered one of these online."

"If I had months to wait for results, I would've," Navid said, ripping open the cotton swab and swiping the inside of his cheeks.

"I'm assuming you want me to keep your results between us so your secret doesn't get out."

He packed up the test and handed it to her. "I told you, I'm a human being. If it's keepin' you up at night, my results should ease your mind."

"Are you sure?"

He sighed. "Yes, Pen. I'm perfectly normal, just..."

"Possessed?"

"No."

"Dad a demon?"

"Not an *actual* demon."

"What are you then? Because what I saw the other day was anything but *normal*."

"I'm," He stopped, unsure of just how honest he should be with her. On one hand, she was helping him and probably deserved to know after what he'd put her through recently. On the other hand, he knew how absurd it sounded. But, after what she witnessed, was it really that far-fetched? "Cursed."

She laughed. "Cursed? Like, by a witch?"

"Sort of but she was bein' manipulated by..."

She stifled a giggle. "By what?"

He blew out a raspberry knowing how ridiculous what he was about to say would sound. "God."

She burst out laughing, clutching her stomach and dabbing her eyes. "Well, you're full of yourself, ain't ya?"

"Just run the DNA, all right? See if you can find any relatives. They'd be distant. *Real* distant. It's a long shot but it's the only shot I've got."

"You trying to see if any of them are *cursed* like you?"

"Not *exactly* like me."

"I'll run it but Navid, cursed by God? Really?"

"That's what they tell me."

"Who?"

"Would you believe an angel?"

She pursed her lips. "Do you need to speak to someone at Police Care?"

"Just run the DNA, Pen. Thanks."

"All right but seriously, if you need to talk to someone," She put her hand on his knee, her features softening. An uncomfortable twinge ran up his leg, his instinct telling him to bat it away. That would be rude, he thought but after what Gabriel said about her still having feelings for him, the last thing he wanted to do was give her the wrong idea by letting her touch him like that. It was clear to him now, the way she looked at him, the way she fussed. He had to nip this in the bud without letting her know that he was aware of it and *without* hurting her feelings.

He put his hand over hers and gave it a squeeze. "We're friends, aren't we, Pen?"

She paused, swallowing hard before answering, "We are."

"So I can count on you to keep this quiet, yeah?"

"Of course."

"Because I have a wife, a family depending on me. People I care about. This secret can't get out. Nothing can threaten my family, you understand?"

She pulled her hand away, nodding and clearing her throat. "I understand. I won't tell anyone."

"Thank you."

"Course." She got up from her seat on the sofa and headed to the door. "I'll put a rush on it but it'll still be a while. Will you be all right here in the meantime?"

"I don't have a choice, do I?"

"You always have a choice, Navid." She looked around at Giovanni's living room, avoiding eye contact. "Seems you've made yours." She left the flat, closing the door softly behind her.

He fell back onto the couch, relieved the conversation had only been mildly unpleasant .

Two weeks went by with no word from Pen. He knew DNA testing took time but he was going crazy not being with Phindi. What if she went into labor early? He should be with her. She needed him.

His phone buzzed on the coffee table and for a brief moment, hope that it was Pen with results fluttered his stomach. Looking at the screen, he was deflated. "Hey, Gran, " he answered.

"I spoke to Gabriel, *finally*. Are you all right?"

"Yeah, just itching to get home."

"That's the last thing you want to do, believe me."

"Why? If I go home, what happens?"

"You will die. Painfully."

"Yeah, but I'll just come back, won't I? So--"

"Yes, you would come back and seven minutes later, you would die again in a pool of your own blood and sick. Seven minutes after that, you'd come back again, and so on and so on. Believe me, Cain tested it...repeatedly."

"Right, but--"

"Listen to me, Navid. I watched my father suffer with this for thirty-one years before he abandoned me. Each death left its mark, left him angrier, crueler. He was tortured and broken and I will not allow that to happen to you."

He could hear her attempting to hide the quiver in her voice, the sound flooding him with guilt. "I'm sorry, Gran. I didn't mean to upset you."

"I'm not upset, I am *right*. Do as Gabriel instructs and keep out of London until the curse is lifted."

"What if it never is? What kind of father will I be always on the move? Can't build a home, put down roots. What if I'm stuck like this for thousands of years like Cain was?"

"You will not be," she said so matter-of-factly, he almost believed it.

He shook his head. "You don't know that. She told you what I have to do, right? Track down cousins three hundred times removed. It's impossible"

"It's not."

"But--"

"This is one of Elohim's plans and while I have issues with him, he always gets what he wants. If he's entrusted you with a task, you will accomplish it."

"Now you sound like Gabriel."

"I find that hard to believe."

"She said she believed in me. It sounded snarky comin' out of her mouth but I think she meant it."

"Of course, she did. She knows better than anyone what it means to be one of God's chess pieces."

"Hmm."

"Trust yourself, your instincts. He chose you for a reason."

"Thanks, Gran. I'll do my best."

"That's all you've got to do. I love you, Navid. Be careful."

"Love you, too, Gran." He ended the call and rolled his head back, his feelings of helplessness and worry driving him crazy. There had to be *something* he could do while he waited for the DNA to come back.

He was shaken from his melancholy by a knock on the door. It couldn't be Giovanni. He wouldn't knock on his own door. If it was the police again he didn't know if he had the energy or ability to lie to them the way Gabriel had. He thought about ignoring it but a few seconds later, more knocking came, harder than before. He stood and moved to the door, hoping whoever it was would be easily gotten rid of.

An auburn-haired woman with light eyes wearing a perfume that smelled of lilies stood in the hall. "Is Giovanni in?" she asked, wringing her hands.

"No, sorry," he told her. "He's out of town at the moment."

"Oh, um, are you his...partner?"

"His...no."

"Oh. I thought you might be like, an assistant or something. I'm Cat. I was hoping he might have work for me. See, I've been," she paused, shame coloring her features. "Away. But, now that I'm back, I need to make money. Do you know when he'll be back?"

"Not for a while, I think. Sorry, love." He began to close the door but she threw her palm against it, holding it open.

"Sorry but have we met?"

"I don't think so. I was here a few years ago for a night. You might've seen me then but I don't remember you, I'm sorry."

"A few years ago." She stared, her eyes going from slits to saucers, her face going ghost white."

"You all right?"

"I," She backed away. "I have to go." She bolted down the hall, her heels on the marble floor clicking like a typewriter.

"Okay..." He started to close the door but before it could latch, she was back, cheeks flushed and eyes wild.

"You're real?" She accused, anger tinting her voice.

"I'm..." He tilted his head in confusion. *"Yeah.* What--"

"Do you know someone named Cain? Or Lilith?"

He glanced around the hall to make sure no one had heard before pulling her inside and closing the door. "How do you know them?"

"They're real too, aren't they?" She looked terrified, like she was hoping he would say anything but yes.

"Yeah, they're real. Dead now but real."

Tears pooled in her eyes as she began to shake. "I--I'm sorry, I need to sit." She shuffled to the sofa and sat, hugging her arms and rocking back and forth, her expression going from afraid to angry.

He sat next to her, gently touching her shoulder. "What did they do to you, love?"

Tears tumbled down her now flaming cheeks, her eyes on the floor. "I spent four years in the bin thinkin' I was cracked, thinkin' I was a murderer, bein' told I'd had a psychotic break and you're tellin' me it was all real? Bible characters slaughterin' people, bangin' on trains." She gestured to him. "Puttin' hexes on bonnie lads, fightin' demons in the desert?"

"By all accounts, that does sound like them, yeah."

She jumped up, racing to the kitchen sink, and throwing up in it. She rinsed out her mouth and the porcelain, leaning on the counter for support.

"You all right?"

She shook her head. "What that crazy bitch did, made me do." More tears came as she covered her mouth. When she removed it, she said something that made his skin crawl. *"Made me eat."*

He thought he might vomit, too, knowing what Lilith's preferred snacks were. "She possessed you," he realized. "I'm so sorry."

"But, you seem all right." She walked back to stand next to the sofa, looking down at him with hopeful eyes. "So, it didn't work? The curse switch?"

"Oh, it worked," he said, standing to look her in the eye. "But, I'm all right. I have help."

"Gabriel?"

"For starters."

"She was worried about her. Scared, even. It's good, you havin' an angel in your pocket. Better, at least than havin' one in your head."

"She goes there, too, but not like Lilith. I'm sorry. What was done to you, it's horrifying."

"Fucked up is what it is. Epically, unconscionably, and majorly fucked up."

"Agreed."

She took a few calming breaths, not that it seemed to help. He could see she was still trembling. "Sorry for boakin' in your sink. Er, Giovanni's sink."

"Don't be. I've been there. Recently."

"I need to go process." She headed to the door and he followed her.

"Of course. Will you be all right?"

She spun around to look up at him, fresh tears brimming. "You said they're dead? Like, *dead,* dead?"

He put his hand on her shoulder, his tone reassuring and his expression kind but serious. "I have it on good authority Cain's in Limbo and Lilith's in a maximum security wing of Hell. They won't hurt you again, or anyone *ever.*"

She nodded, her lip quivering as her tears spilled. She threw her arms around his waist, sobbing into his chest and holding on to him like hope.

"It's all right, love," he said, petting her hair, feeling so sorry for her that he forgot for a moment all of his own problems. "You're safe now."

Chapter 13

A NOTHER WEEK WENT BY, Navid piddling around Giovanni's flat, ordering enough food to feed a family every day and sleeping more than he had in years. He filled his waking hours with telly and phone calls to his wife, neither calming his nerves nor tamping down the profound sense of urgency he felt with every day that went by without any progress being made. Just when he thought he might lose his mind completely, the phone rang.

"Pen," he answered, a flicker of hope igniting in his chest. "My results in?"

"They are," she said, her tone calmer than the last time they'd spoken. "Congratulations, you are, in fact, human."

"I never actually doubted that, Pen."

"Well, I did."

He rolled his eyes, deciding to ignore the remark. "Any relatives?"

"Just two and just barely. They're both a less than zero point five percent match."

"Good enough."

"One is a twenty-two-year-old playboy in Los Angeles. Son of a recently dead film producer, calls himself an entrepreneur but far as I can tell, the only thing he's done work-wise is invest his trust fund money into other people's businesses. Rum, video games, a sock line. All ventures failed."

"An entitled prick blowin' through his daddy's money. Got it. And his brother?"

She was quiet for a moment, the sound of her typing all he could hear on the other end of the call. "Doesn't have one."

"So, it's not him. What about the other one?"

"Now, *he's* interesting. Rap sheet long as the Thames. Petty theft, a handful of assaults. And, get this, he's got ties to the Cosa Nostra in Sicily. He's pretty high up in rank, too from the looks of it. Not exactly someone I'd recommend invitin' to the family reunion."

"And, his brother?"

Again, she typed. "No record of one but you know how secretive the Mob is."

"I do." Relief washed over him, hope setting in for the first time in weeks. It was too much of a coincidence, his father taking a trip to Italy just as his curse was triggered. It was part of God's plan, he knew it. "Email me everything you've got on both of these guys just in case but I'm pretty sure the Mob boss is my guy. Thanks, Pen." He ended the call, eager to track down his Italian cousin and get the curse-breaking show on the road.

He called Giovanni from the airport, his father agreeing to pick him up and take him to dinner. He took him to his favorite restaurant in Rome, the two eating bowls of Carbonara and sipping wine in silence until Giovanni finally addressed the elephant in the room.

"I heard about the visit the police made. I apologize if they made you uncomfortable."

He kept his eyes on his food as he attempted to sound nonchalant. "It's fine. They took off pretty quick after discovering I'm a detective."

"Ah, good. Still, they shouldn't have bothered you. It's my fault. I knew they might be coming, I just thought there was more time."

"Mm, hmm."

He sighed, dropping his fork. "I am sorry, Navid. I should not have put you in a position to be questioned."

He took a bite of his pasta, still avoiding eye contact. "It's all right."

"No, it's not. I should have sent you to a hotel. I should have--"

"I said, it's all right," he told him, a twinge of irritation in his voice as he tried and failed to keep his feelings about what his father did for a living to himself.

"Navid, look at me."

Reluctantly, he returned his gaze, his features stern.

"I know you disapprove of me, of what I do."

"I didn't say that."

"You didn't have to. It is clear. I won't bore you with why it is I do what I do, the way I grew up, the circumstances that led me to this profession. I also won't defend myself, tell you of all the ways I help and protect my employees. The health screenings I provide. The safe environment in which I give them to work. The money it takes to run my business. The time."

He bit his tongue, wanting to scoff but realizing there was a bit of truth in what he said.

"It's not your concern. What I hope *will* be of interest to you is the fact that I've retired."

"Retired?"

"Yes. I've made enough money that I no longer have to work, you see. I'm thinking of staying here in Italy forever. It's peaceful, wouldn't you agree?"

He shrugged.

"You forget how much home means to you until you return to it. Being away so long, it was like some part of me was missing. Being back has made me feel...whole."

His eyes dropped, the yearning for his wife causing his breath to hitch.

"Such a serious face. What is it, my boy?"

"Just missin' the wife. Baby's comin' soon."

"Baby? Why didn't you say? Waiter," he motioned for the server. "A bottle of Prosecco! My son is about to be a father!"

Light applause and a few shouts of, "Congratulations" erupted from the other patrons as the server nodded and went to fetch a bottle. He brought it along with two champagne flutes to the table, offering his own, "Congratulations" before heading off to attend to other tables.

"If your wife is soon to deliver, what are you doing here? You should be home, tending to her."

"I would love to but there's somethin' I've got to do here first."

"What could be more important than awaiting the arrival of your first bambino?"

He couldn't answer honestly so he simply said, "Work."

"Work?" He took a sip of his drink. "*Work*? Now, I know I'm not exactly father of the year and you have every right to ignore me completely but let me tell you one thing. Had I known you existed, I would have been there. I would have showered you with affection and anything else you required. I would have *loved you* even more than I do now."

He wasn't convinced and his face showed it.

"I'm serious. A child is a blessing from God. You should savor every moment. I was robbed of my time with you. You should not give up yours with your child voluntarily."

"I'll be there for his birth," he stated, knowing he might be lying but hoping it was true.

"His?" A broad smile lit up the older man's face. "A son for my son!"

Again, the restaurant cheered.

Flickers of emotion sparked in his chest, feelings he didn't have time to explore. He shook them from his mind, deciding to get on with the real reason he was there. "Does the name Salvatore Amato ring any bells?"

His face fell, the joy in his eyes fading to fear. "Where did you hear that name?"

"You know him?"

"Only by reputation. I know you're poliziotto but trust me, my boy, you want nothing to do with Sal Amato. He's," He looked around nervously, lowering his voice to just above a whisper. "*Connected.*"

"Yeah, I know."

"He's avoided prison for decades and it's not because he isn't guilty, hmm? Do you understand what I'm saying?"

"I'm not lookin' to bust him. I'm actually here to protect him, believe it or not."

He scoffed. "Protect him? Navid, my boy, if you knew anything about him you'd realize how ridiculous that sounds. The man is more protected than an endangered species."

"My intel says otherwise."

"Why should you protect someone like that, anyhow? Have you any idea what he's done? What he is?"

"It doesn't matter," he explained as best he could. "It's somethin' I've got to do and *before* my son comes."

He sighed, gulping down the last of his wine and flashing a concerned glance. "As you wish. He spends most of his time in Palermo. I can send someone to escort you once you're in the city."

"Escort me?"

"Of course. You can't make your own introduction."

"Why not?"

He offered a puzzled glare before answering. "That's not how it works. If you're uninvited, you must be introduced by someone he respects. Someone that can protect *you*."

"I can handle myself."

"Please, Navid. You don't know these people. I do. Accept my help in this. It's the least I can do after what you endured because of my absence."

"The officers only asked like, two questions. I'm fine."

"That's not what I meant."

They stared at each other for a few moments, understanding hovering like a cloud between them. "Fine," Navid said, taking his last bite of pasta. "As long as this 'help' doesn't get in my way."

Chapter 14

T HE NEXT MORNING, NAVID called Phindi from his Palermo hotel room, explaining where he was and what he was doing there. Surprisingly, she didn't seem that worried, saying she trusted in Elohim's plan for him. He only wished he was as confident.

After the call, he showered and put on a pair of slacks and a light blue button-down, snacking on mini bar pistachios while he waited for his guide. Finally, at a little after nine, a knock came on the door.

"Navid La Rosa?" a suited man asked when he answered.

"Navid *Parsi*," he corrected.

The man pursed his lips, his expression that of condescension and disbelief. "My mistake. I'm Angelo. Your father sent me."

Angelo, he thought. *Of course, that's his name*. He remembered Gabriel once telling him how funny God could be, how much he liked a good pun. The irony was so thick, he almost choked on it. "Come in."

Angelo looked to be in his mid to late twenties, his short hair neatly combed, his suit tailored to perfection. His brows were as thick as his accent and he wasted no time with polite chit-chat. Instead, he looked him over, his amber eyes narrowing in disapproval. "Is that what you're wearing?"

He looked down at himself, suddenly feeling self-conscious. "What's wrong with it?"

"Are you serious?" He sighed, taking his phone from his breast pocket and making a call. "Ho bisogno di un abito alla stanza duecentotre' in albergo su Salita Partanna." He held the phone away from his ear to address Navid in English. "You're a thirty-eight regular, right?"

"Yeah, how'd you--"

He went back to his call. "Trentotto regolari. E scarpe," He paused, looking down at Navid's feet. "Taglia dodici." He ended the call and turned his attention back to Navid. "Have you eaten?"

"Just this." He held out the half-eaten bag of nuts.

Angelo shook his head, poking his head out into the hall and waving down a bellboy. He whispered into the young man's ear, the latter nodding and hurrying off.

"Do I want to know what you do for work, Angelo?" Navid asked.

"I very much doubt it."

"Would you tell me if I asked?"

"No."

He bit the inside of his cheek, deciding it best not to get any more involved in mafia business than he absolutely had to. He was there for a reason and it wasn't to get killed by trying to take down the entire Cosa Nostra alone. "Fair enough."

Soon, the bellboy was back pushing a cart carrying coffee, fruit, and croissants. Angelo tipped the young man, patting his back as he left. He moved to the window and peeked outside, seeming satisfied by whatever he saw. "Mangiare. I'll be just outside." He went into the hall and closed the door behind him, giving Navid privacy to eat in peace.

He sat on the edge of the bed, sipping dark roast and eating quickly, looking forward to getting his meeting with his mobster cousin over with. With any luck, he'd get the name of his brother, track him down, and find a reason to lock him up thereby saving Sal and ending his curse. He felt it a little ridiculous that he, a decorated, not to mention immortal detective was being escorted by what felt like a bodyguard to visit a criminal but it was kind of nice that Giovanni offered. After their conversation the day before, he was beginning to think maybe his father really did care about him, at least a little.

In his new suit, his shoes pinching and the caffeine in his coffee working its magic, Navid followed Angelo to a few of Sal's known haunts. They found him just before noon, holding court at a small restaurant overlooking the Tyrrhenian Sea, sitting alone at the only outdoor table, sipping a glass of red wine. Four men in black suits stood a few feet away forming a perimeter. Whether they were guards, henchmen, or both, they didn't look like men to be trifled with.

As they got closer, Navid took in Sal's appearance and general demeanor, assessing him as a potential combatant, as he did most people upon first meeting them, a habit learned on the job he couldn't seem to shake. While sitting, it was hard to make an exact determination of height but he guessed Sal was about six-four, built like a Mac truck with a receding hairline and sharp jaw. What hair he did have was jet black and slicked back, obviously dyed and coated in too much product. He had deep forehead wrinkles and crow's feet, wine-stained lips, and a gold pinky ring with the letter A engraved on its head. With his legs crossed he could see bright purple socks covering his ankle, a cue to him that he either didn't take himself too seriously or that he considered himself royal. He prayed it was option one since option two would make him either delusional or a narcissist.

As they approached, two of Sal's men blocked their path, hands reaching into their jackets, presumably to retrieve weapons Navid was sure they carried. "What's this?" Sal asked, setting his glass on the small, iron and glass table.

Navid opened his mouth to speak but Angelo held his hand out to stop him, instead speaking himself. "We've come to offer protection."

All five men laughed, Sal taking another sip from his glass. "Do I look to be in need of protection?" He put his glass down and looked them over, addressing his men. "Who is this guy?"

The man directly in front of Angelo answered, "You know Angelo, Matteo's boy."

"Ah, yes, the butcher."

Angelo nodded respectfully.

"And, this one?" Sal asked, gesturing to Navid who had run out of patience.

"I have it on good authority that your life is in danger."

Angelo smacked his shoulder while the other men laughed again. Sal poured himself another glass and took a swig before addressing Navid directly. "My life is always in danger." Chugging the rest of the glass, he kept his eyes trained on him, assessing him, seemingly the way Navid had assessed him. "What are you, English?"

"That's right," he replied.

"He's half Italian," Angelo chimed. "His father's a La Rosa."

"Is that right?" He leaned back in his seat, folding his arms, his approving expression telling Navid there was something about his father that he didn't want him to know. Maybe he, too was "connected" or, at least, used to be. Maybe that was one of the things he'd been referring to at dinner the night before when he mentioned "how he grew up". It would certainly explain how he'd been able to secure Angelo for babysitting duty. "So, an Italian Englishman has come all the way here because he thinks I'm in danger. And, from whom did you come by this information?"

"That's not important."

"I beg to differ, Englishman. In my experience, information is only as good as its source."

"It's credible, believe me."

"Mmm. And, who is it that you think is trying to kill me today?"

"Not sure. A brother, most likely."

Again, the men laughed, Sal holding a hand up for them to stop so he could speak, which they did. "Well, that's the problem, isn't it? While I have no siblings by blood, everyone here is someone I consider a brother, save you, of course. So, which is it?" He gestured to the men around him, mockery in his tone. "Which of my fratelli is poised for betrayal?"

From afar, Navid inspected the men. The two in front of him were calm, their shoulders relaxed, and their lips turned up in weakly hidden smirks. The man to Sal's left was equally dismissive, checking his watch and looking bored. The man to his right, however, had beads of sweat forming at his temples, tight muscles even in his jaw, and sported a smile so fake he was surprised he was the only one who noticed. Without hesitation, Navid pointed him out. "Safe money's on him."

"You can't be serious," the guilty man said, voice shaking. "I wouldn't," He turned to face Sal. "You know I'd never try anything stupid."

Sal looked him in the eye, then at Navid, then back at him. He stood, his lumbering frame casting a shadow on the much shorter mobster. "I want to believe you, Enzo. I really do. But, the Englishman seems pretty sure."

"I--" Enzo shuffled backward, his eyes wide with fear. After a few seconds, his features became rigid. "You know what?" He reached for his gun. "Fanculo."

"Gun!" Navid shouted, pushing past the two men in his way and throwing himself between Sal and Enzo, knocking the mob boss to the ground and covering him with his body. The man to Sal's left sprung into action, taking several shots at Enzo who had barely gotten his gun from its holster and was attempting to run. The guards chased him down, disarming him and dragging him back to the front of the building.

"Take him inside," Sal commanded as he and Navid stood, brushing the street dirt from their suits.

"You all right?" Angelo asked, hurrying to clean off the back of Sal's jacket.

"I'm fine," he grunted, turning his attention to Navid. "Who told you Enzo was planning on taking me out?"

"Call them an angel," he replied.

Sal laughed again, this time louder, his cheeks reddening. "I love this guy. Come, have lunch with me."

"I don't think that's--"

Angelo kicked him in the ankle, reminding him of how important manners were to people like this. Navid offered a small smile. "All right."

They went inside the dimly lit restaurant, a tiny six-table establishment run by a woman in her sixties. She brought them a bottle of Etna Rosso as they sat, Sal facing the door, watching as the other men hauled Enzo to a room behind the counter. Angelo sat opposite with Navid between, uncomfortably close to the giant mob boss. Within moments, Navid could hear the screams, cries of a man being tortured. His body tensed, the desire to put an end to Enzo's suffering gnawing at him as the woman brought out plates of Caponata.

"Do you know," Sal said, clapping him on the back. "I had you clocked as poliziotto. I was *this close* to having you...handled. But, you saved my life. Pula or not, you have my respect." He held his glass out, Navid clinking his glass to it. "Mangiare, mangiare," he said, gesturing to Navid's plate and picking up his fork.

As the men ate, more screams sounded from the back room, Navid's willpower wearing thin. It took everything in him not to arrest everyone there, to end the torture that was going on not fifty feet away. But, he was one cop surrounded by armed mafiosi. He was outnumbered, outgunned, and if he'd done his job, a death here would be his last. Better to play along, ignore what was happening behind closed doors, and get safely back to Phindi.

Chapter 15

N AVID BREATHED A SIGH of relief as he sat in the passenger side of Angelo's Fiat, the two escaping the awkward lunch with Sal relatively unscathed. Driving back to the hotel, the weight of his curse lifted, he couldn't help but smile. It was over.

"You did well," Angelo said, keeping his eyes on the road. "That could have gone very badly but you held yourself together. Well done."

"Held myself together?" Navid asked. "What do you mean?"

"You don't have to pretend with me. I know who you are."

His throat went dry. Was Angelo more than an ironically named gangster? Was he one of them? An angel? "Wha--what do you mean?"

"I looked you up, *detective*."

Another wave of relief washed over him. "Oh."

"Taking down the Mare Boys almost single-handedly is quite im-pressive. I was surprised Sal hadn't heard of you. He usually keeps up with these things."

"What things?"

He gave him a sideways glance before returning his gaze to the road ahead. "Potential threats."

"I'm a potential threat?"

"Apparently, not. You saved his life. Odd thing for someone like you to do."

"I didn't have much choice."

"Mmm. I apologize if I offended you, calling you by your father's surname. I thought it would be...a disguise of sorts. An internet search of Navid La Rosa would turn up nothing but had he looked up Navid Parsi, as I did, you could have been in trouble."

"Oh," he said, embarrassed he hadn't caught on before now. "Well, thanks for havin' my back."

"Think nothing of it. I owed Giovanni a favor. This makes us square."

"Should I ask why you owed him?"

He tilted his head slightly, his expression unchanging. "No."

"Probably for the best. After I pick up my things, would you mind giving me a lift to the airport? I'm eager to get home to my wife."

He was silent for a moment, his face still.

"Angelo?"

"It's not my place to meddle. If you wish to leave Italy without saying goodbye to your father, that's up to you."

"I'll text him."

"You'll..." He bit his lip, a crease forming between his dark brows. "It's not my business, of course, but it's not right to disrespect your father in this way. He deserves more from you."

"You think you know what he deserves?"

"I think I know him better than you do."

"Is that so? Do you know what he does for a living? How he cheats those girls?"

"What a man does for money is not who he is. We all do things we'd rather not to provide for ourselves and those who depend on us. What's in a man's soul is what matters. How he loves. He loves you, his son, whether you take his name or not. But, as I said, it's not my business."

He felt like a petulant child, pouting in the passenger seat of another man's car, scowl on his face, fighting to keep his lips from forming a pout. Maybe he *was* being immature, reckless with his father's feelings. Maybe he did owe him a face-to-face goodbye, especially since he didn't know when or even if he'd see him again. He had helped him to break his curse, though he didn't know it. He simply helped him because he asked. "Fine. We can stop by on the way to the airport."

Angelo lifted his lips in a half-smile and nodded.

They arrived at Giovanni's home in the Lazio countryside where he had prepared a feast to celebrate his son's victory in protecting Salvatore and the upcoming birth of his first child. He had grilled meats, various pastas, and bruschetta, copious amounts of wine, and panettone for dessert. They ate outside at a small picnic table under twinkling lights and a blanket of stars, La Traviata playing quietly from a portable speaker.

"This opera always breaks my heart," Giovanni said, swirling his glass. "Is there anything worse than doomed love?"

"I could think of a few things," Navid muttered, remembering the sting of death, the vampires' torture, and the guilt he felt while listening to Enzo being beaten while he did nothing to help him.

"Yes, I imagine in your line of work, you've seen things I could not fathom. Still, losing a great love to something out of one's control, I can not think of anything more tragic." He put his glass down and looked him in the eye. "It's true, I did not love your mother. I only knew her for a short time and that's my fault. At twenty I was even more irresponsible than I am now, if you can believe it. Desperate to break free of the life I was born into, wild, blowing off steam at every opportunity. Your mother was beautiful, sexy,"

"That's enough, I think."

"No, you must hear this." He leaned forward, hands folded on the table. "For an all too brief period of time, your mother made me forget who I was, who I was supposed to be. She was exhilarating. Being with her was like breathing for the first time. I felt real joy when I was with her, a thing I'd not experienced before. I spent thirty years chasing that feeling only to come by it again when you discovered me." He grabbed Navid's hand and held it tightly, not breaking eye contact. "I know you think me repulsive but what I did was necessary, believe me. The alternative was far worse. And, now, I'm free. I can live as I see fit, here, away from..."

"From what?"

"It doesn't matter. My point is, my life is far better with you in it and I hope, someday, now that I've given up my...work, that you might see fit to visit more often. To include me in your family. If you don't, I will understand. I've given you no reason to trust me but--"

"No," he said, taking his hand away, his heart warming. "I don't need to hear any more. I don't like what you did, takin' advantage of those girls, takin' their money. But, I also don't know what you went through to get to that point. If today has taught me anything it's that people do all kinds of stuff they wouldn't normally do when they feel they've got no choice. Means to an end doesn't justify everything but you have shown me kindness. It's only fair I do the same."

Tears welled in the older man's eyes, his features lifting.

"Maybe I could come back in a few months when the baby can travel."

He gasped.

"It's only right you should meet your grandson and more importantly, it would be good for my son to have more family. He shouldn't be deprived of a grandfather, especially one that can cook like this." He grinned, taking a bite of his dessert.

"My boy!" He leaned forward, taking his face in his hands and kissing his cheeks. "You've made me happier than I can tell you. Oh, it'll be wonderful! I'll take him on a tour of Rome, the Colosseum, the fountains. So much history I can teach him! We'll go for gondola rides in Venice, take a day tour of Florence. We'll go to the opera, museums."

"Gettin' a little ahead of yourself, aren't you?"

"On the contrary! I should start preparations now. Everything I didn't get to do with you as a boy, everything I missed, we can now do as a family. Oh, my son!" He kissed his cheeks again, tears of joy spilling from his eyes. "You will not regret this. What you've given me is a gift and I will cherish it, always."

His heart swelled, his father's glee proving contagious. As Navid's gaze drifted to Angelo asleep in a nearby hammock, he realized he'd been right. Whatever Giovanni had done in the past, he *had* helped him, he *did* care for him, and he *was* his father. It had only taken a run-in with the mafia, a lecture from a gangster, and a heartfelt speech to make him finally feel like it.

Chapter 16

L OOKING THROUGH THE PRIVATE jet's window down at the English Channel, Navid could hardly contain his excitement. He was on his way home, finally, to his wife and his soon-to-be-born son *and* with a repaired relationship with his father. The trip couldn't have gone better, save the gut-wrenching sounds of Enzo getting his ass kicked. But, he *had* been planning on killing someone, and in that world of gangsters and murderers, what happened to him was justified. Had it been up to him, he'd be rotting in a cell instead of being beaten within an inch of his life and banished from the country forever but at least they hadn't killed him so he let his guilt drift away, replaced by the sweet bliss of coming home.

As the plane approached land, he felt a strange tingling in his legs. He had been sitting for over two hours so pins and needles were to be expected. He stood, pacing the cabin to improve circulation. But soon, the needles became knives, stabbing at his nerves like a fork into meat. The pain rose to his abdomen, like chains around his waist, nausea not far behind. *What the fuck*, he thought. *This shouldn't be happening. It's meant to be over.*

"Are you all right, sir?" the sole flight attendant asked as he put a hand to his chest, his heart rate speeding out of control.

"Turn it 'round," he said, holding back a cough.

"Excuse me, sir?"

"Turn the plane around." He dropped to his knees in front of her.

"Sir, what's wrong?!"

"Please," He coughed, the taste of copper filling his mouth. "Turn the bloody plane around!"

"Yes, sir," she said, backing away, panic in her eyes as she turned and scurried to the cockpit.

He doubled over, waves of nausea and pain like fire overtaking all other senses. "Not again," he grunted, falling forward, not feeling his head hit the floor, going unconscious yet again.

He came to as the plane made its descent at the Grand Calais Airport in Marck, France. After landing, the flight attendant came out of the cockpit, stopping in her tracks at the sight of him, blood on his chin, skin ashen as he stood on wobbly legs.

"Forgive me, sir," she said, helping him to his seat. "I thought you'd..."

"Died?"

She cleared her throat, averting her glance. "I'm sorry, sir. You were just so still after your collapse."

"It's all right, love," he told her, sitting back, hardly able to keep his eyes open. "It's happened before. Just a...genetic condition. I'll be all right after I get some food in me."

"Of course, sir." She rushed to fetch him something from her cart. "Turkey and Swiss." She handed him the plastic-wrapped sandwich and a tin of water. "Will this do?"

"Yes, thank you."

She offered a polite smile and hurried away, leaving him to eat alone. The small meal was not enough to satiate him, as he knew it would not be, but it was better than nothing. As he swallowed the last bit of his sandwich, his eyes drooping and his head pounding, he tried to make sense of how he remained afflicted. Enzo had been planning on killing Sal. He tried to pull a gun on him. He saved his cousin's life. The curse should have been lifted. So, why hadn't it?

He got off the plane, so weary he almost forgot his bag and leaned against the building, the letters above him spelling out Calais-Dunkerque in crimson. Sitting on the ground, he took his phone from his pocket and called Pen.

"Navid," she answered, hope in her voice he chose to ignore.

"Hey, Pen. How sure are you that I'm related to Salvatore Amato?"

"As sure as one can be about such things. Test shows point zero five percent shared paternal DNA."

He froze. "Did you say, paternal?"

"Yeah, why?"

"Fuckin' hell."

"What's wrong?"

"Nothing. And, what about the kid in L.A.?"

"Same thing, point zero five percent shared DNA."

His heart sank, afraid to hear the answer to the question he had to ask. "Paternal?"

"No, that one's on the maternal side."

"Oh, thank God."

"Is everythin' all right?"

"No," he said, getting to his feet. "But, it will be. Thanks, Pen." He ended the call, rolling his neck and sighing. "Looks like I'm going to the States."

Once again in the jet Allydia had chartered for him, he began putting the puzzle pieces together. His father making his home in a foreign country for decades, making his money illegally, the talk of his youth, how desperate he was to get away from the life he was born into. The look of approval on Sal's face when he heard the name La Rosa. They were related, whether they knew it or not, and Giovanni had undoubtedly been raised in the same kind of environment Sal had been. He was born into the Cosa Nostra.

Shoveling bag after bag of crisps down his gullet, he had a new-found respect for his father. What it must have taken to get out of that life, how hard it must have been. And, now, finally, he was free. "Good for him," he said under his breath. His father had escaped the curse he'd been born into. Now, it was his turn to do the same.

Chapter 17

"One Museum Square," Navid told the cab driver, squinting in the glaring Los Angeles sun as he closed the car door and set his bag next to him on the worn seat.

"British?" the driver asked, pulling away from the curb.

"Yeah."

"It's a pretty accent," he said, keeping his eyes on the road as they left the airport's parking lot. "Terrible food, though."

He was mildly insulted but kept it to himself.

"What do you think of L.A. so far?"

"It's bright," he said, the hunger and fatigue keeping him honest. "Oppressively sunny, like the weather's demanding you be in a good mood."

He laughed, flashing bleached teeth under a well-groomed mustache. "You in town long?"

"I hope not," he said, realizing instantly how rude it sounded. "I'm here on business," he told him, hoping to avoid offending the driver, though *he'd* had no problem insulting his whole country with that "terrible food" comment. "The sooner I get it done, the sooner I can get back to my wife."

"Oh, I know how that goes. My last movie had me filming in Canada for a three months. Missed my anniversary. Still haven't lived it down."

"You're an actor?"

"Buddy, this is L.A. Everyone's an actor."

He chuckled under his breath.

"What do you do?"

"I'm a detective."

"Oh?"

He noticed the driver glancing at the glove compartment through the rear view mirror. He was obviously hiding something in there he didn't want found but it was no concern of his. He was there for one reason and one reason only and it wasn't to bust a cabbie stashing drugs in his work vehicle.

The driver quickly changed the subject. "If you'll be in town for a few days, you should check out the local cuisine. A new place just opened up on Santa Monica. Best steak in town, or so I hear. Sinclair's."

"Oh, I know the owner of that place," he realized.

"You do?"

"Yeah, he's my Gran's stepson."

He pulled over, stopping in front of Allydia's Miracle Mile apartment building. He turned in his seat, his eyes wide with excitement. "You know Will Sinclair? Personally?"

Confused by the driver's enthusiasm, he simply replied, "Um, yeah."

"*The* Will Sinclair? Famous restaurateur from New York, Will Sinclair?"

"I didn't realize he was famous but, yeah."

"You think you could get me a table?"

"Uh..."

"If I could take my girl to Sinclair's on a Saturday night, she'd one hundred percent forgive me. I'd get so many brownie points."

"Um..."

"I won't charge you for the ride," he said, wide eyes pleading. "In fact," he took a headshot from the passenger seat and handed it to him. "My number's on the back. Call me any time you need a ride while you're here and I'll drive you, free of charge."

"All right, I guess." He took his phone from his pocket and texted Will, a legal relation he'd only spoken to a handful of times but who'd always seemed nice enough. "What's your name?"

"Topher Alexander."

He waited for a response, Topher's hopeful stare making him slightly uncomfortable. Finally, Will texted back, *Sure, I'll let the manager know to expect him plus one Saturday at eight.* He relayed the message, Topher nearly squealing with glee.

"Oh, my God, thank you! Becca aside, do you have any idea what this will do for my career? Being seen at Sinclair's is basically like walking a red carpet. Everyone who's anyone will be there. This is amazing. Seriously, man, thank you."

"No problem." He got out of the cab, duffel in hand, and made his way to the apartment Allydia occasionally rented out, the former vampire keeping to the East Coast as much as possible. Upon entering, he was immediately struck by how fancy it was. So fancy that he felt out of place, like he'd stepped onto a movie set. Everything was either bright white or stainless steel, every exterior wall made entirely of glass. The view was spectacular, the city below and mountains in the distance. The massive balcony housed a large grill, two chaise lounge chairs and a sectional sofa made of wicker and canvas, a fire table, and a dining table with six chairs that matched the other outdoor furniture.

He wandered around the thirteen-hundred-square-foot apartment, more impressed with every room he entered. "Bloody hell," he muttered at the sight of the huge shower and double sinks in the master bath, the back-lit mirror showing him just how blown away he was. If he was going to be taken seriously by people with this kind of money, he'd have to dress to impress. Thankfully, Angelo had let him keep the suit.

He steamed the wrinkles from it and hung it in the master closet before parking himself at the desk in the office and opening the laptop. There, he began his research. "Ian Berman," he said as he typed. "What have you gotten up to?" It was as Pen had told him. His father had died about a year before, he'd inherited his mansion and his money, blowing a ton of it on one failed venture after another. Police had been called to his home a few times but only for noise complaints. Apparently, the boy enjoyed a good party. He was dating a popular Instagram model called Poppy Malone and from what he could tell, lived a life of relative leisure, not hurting anyone. So, with no brothers, who wanted him dead and why?

Digging deeper into his business affairs, he discovered one man whose businesses Ian had dumped millions of dollars into over the past seven months. Three different ventures, all failed within a couple of months. With a little more investigating, he found the man, Miguel Torres had been suspected of financial crimes but was never charged. Maybe Miguel was like a brother to Ian, best friends and business partners. Maybe Miguel blamed Ian and his party boy ways for the businesses failing. It wasn't a lot to go on but he was the closest thing to a suspect he had.

As the sun set, the rosy glow filling the apartment with orange and red light, he ordered a family's amount of food and ate, shoveling bites of bread, salad, and herbed chicken in his mouth faster than he could swallow. He meticulously cleaned up after himself, not wanting to sully the pristine kitchen any more than he had to. When night came, he crashed on Egyptian cotton sheets, so exhausted, that he almost passed out before making it to the bedroom. As his eyes closed, he made plans in his head to meet with Ian in the morning. He only hoped by then it wouldn't be too late.

After a protein-heavy breakfast, Navid suited up and called Topher for a ride to Ian's Beverly Hills mansion, the cabbie keeping his word by not charging him. With no answer at the front door, he walked around to the back yard, a sprawling two acres of manicured shrubbery and concrete, an Olympic-sized pool at the center with a hot tub adjacent. He found Ian lying on a lawn chair, bright blond hair exaggerating his tan. He wore navy swim trunks and sunglasses on top of his head, his girlfriend in the chair next to him scrolling on her phone. Bleached hair was made obvious with dark roots, her green eyes sparkling in the California sun, the heat of its rays making him second guess his choice of attire.

"Ian Berman?" he said, keeping a bit of distance so as not to spook them.

The young man stood, the muscles in his chest tightening telling Navid that his presence made him nervous. "Yes?"

His girlfriend also stood, positioning herself a step behind.

"Detective Navid Parsi," He flashed his warrant card. "Can you tell me the last time you spoke to Miguel Torres?"

"Miguel?" He stepped closer. "Is he all right?"

"Far as I know." He didn't want to drag this conversation out, desperate to get home, so he just came out with it. "I have reason to believe he may be planning on killing you."

Ian laughed, his look of concern fading as fast as it had come. "No way. Miguel's a friend."

Poppy touched his shoulder, her voice quiet. "A cop wouldn't be here if there wasn't a credible threat."

He rolled his eyes. "Miguel would never hurt me. We've been friends since we were six."

His statement made him seem even more guilty as far as Navid was concerned. A lifelong friend was as close to a brother as one could get. "When was the last time you spoke with him?"

"I don't know, a couple of weeks ago, I think."

"And, what was the nature of your conversation?"

"Huh?"

"What did you talk about?"

"I don't think that's any of your business."

"Ian," Poppy whispered.

"No, this is ridiculous. Miguel is my best friend. Besides, he wouldn't hurt a fly."

"Anyone else, then? Another friend, cousin, maybe? Anyone close to you that might be holding a grudge?"

"What? No. I thought this was about Miguel."

With little time and no patience, he resorted to lying...sort of. "I don't want to scare you, Mr. Berman, but a threat has been made on your life by *someone* who considers you a brother. Who else could have made it?"

"A threat?" Ian asked, his suspicious expression and puffed-out chest annoying Navid. The posturing was enough to make him, too roll his eyes. He fought the urge as the other man continued to mock him. "What kind of threat? An email? A letter? Were the words cut from magazines?"

"Ian," Poppy again scolded.

"No, no. I want to hear it. Where are you getting this information?"

She moved to his side, her tone pleading. "He's a cop. Please take this seriously."

"I saw the security cameras out front," Navid said, avoiding the question. "You should have more back here. You're vulnerable."

Ian scoffed. "Not that it's any of your business, but we do things back here we don't necessarily want filmed."

Poppy slapped his arm.

"What about security guards?" he asked, ignoring the innuendo.

"I have a couple come out when I host parties, just in case. Things have been known to get a little wild."

"But, none the rest of the time?"

"An unnecessary expense."

"Apparently not," Poppy said, her voice increasing in volume and clarity. "What about you?"

"What about me?" Navid asked.

"Would you mind? I know detectives aren't usually private security, too but it would make me feel a lot better. Just until we figure this all out?"

"You're being crazy," Ian said. "I haven't received any threats. As far as we know, this guy's a conman looking for a payout."

"I'm not here for money. This is official police business."

"Except you're not police. Not American police, anyway. And, no offense, but your badge looks fake as fuck."

He pressed his tongue to his cheek, agitated and out of fucks to give, he gave them an instruction. "Look me up."

Without hesitation, Poppy began typing on her phone while Ian crossed his arms in defiance. The woman's eyes widened as she read out loud, "Duncan Lawrence, leader of the UK gang, The Mare Boys, was killed in the home of Detective Navid Parsi when he broke in and attacked the Scotland Yard detective and his pregnant wife, Phindi. Parsi survived two gunshot wounds to the chest. Phindi Parsi was unharmed. This comes after a years-long investigation headed by Parsi which led to the arrest of dozens of gang members in the greater London area." She showed the screen to her boyfriend. "He's legit. There's even a picture of him."

Ian's lips pursed, his brows raising as he skimmed the article. "Fine," he said, looking him in the eye. "But, I'm telling you, it's not Miguel."

"You may be right about that," Navid said, sure that he wasn't. "But, until I figure this out, every man you know is a suspect. Make me a list."

"Of *every man I know?*"

"In order of closeness. Friends, relatives, business partners. In the meantime, you shouldn't be out in the open like this. Get inside, lock all the doors and windows. Do you have any weapons in the home?"

"Come on," he complained. "This is excessive."

"This is *your life*," Poppy urged.

"For fuck's sake, fine!" Ian led them inside to the kitchen, closing the patio doors behind them.

Poppy put her phone on the sparkling quartz countertop and opened the fridge. "Have a seat. You hungry?"

Navid sat at the island while Ian stormed through the house and up the stairs. As she gathered ingredients, Navid answered, "Lately, always."

Chapter 18

T WO DAYS WENT BY, Ian complaining constantly about being "locked up" while Poppy spent her time glued to her phone. Navid installed security cameras at the back door and around the property and called local police with the list of names Ian had given him. As he'd suspected, none of them had records. It was clear to him that Miguel was the would-be murderer. He just had to prove it.

After dinner on the third night, Navid was planting himself at the kitchen island, the central point of the first floor with sight lines to both doors, pulling up the security camera feeds on his laptop when he heard Poppy gasp from the living room sofa. He spun in his seat, reaching for the gun on his hip, expecting to need it. Instead, he saw the twenty-year-old model staring with her mouth hanging open at her screen.

"You all right?" he asked, holstering his weapon.

"You're Will Sinclair's nephew?!" she yelped, getting Ian's attention. He'd been sitting in a chair across the room reading on his tablet but was now up from his seat, brow arched as he stood behind her to look at her phone.

"By marriage," Navid said. "Kind of. How do you know that?"

"The guy from *Three Pucks Shy* posted a video from Sinclair's thanking you for being such a great friend." She flipped the screen to show him.

He walked over, glancing at the screen and shaking his head. "I met that guy twice."

"Welcome to L.A.," Ian said with a cynical laugh. "I'm going to bed. You coming?"

Poppy stood, swiping to another video as she followed him up the stairs. "Night!" she called back.

"Goodnight," Navid said, retaking his seat at the island and muttering to himself, "Welcome to L.A., where names are traded like baseball cards and the only real things are the egos." *That's probably not fair*, he thought, knowing that his longing for home, for his wife, was coloring his judgment. His phone buzzed in his pocket with a call from his former boss. "Hey, Pen," he answered.

"Hey, Navid. Do you have a second to talk?" The excitement in her voice caused him to stand.

"Sure. What's happening?"

"While you've been off on your adventure, I've been working on our corruption case."

"Oh? Did you find anything interesting?"

"I did. Navid, it went all the way up to *the mayor*. I have everything I need to bring them all down."

"Are you serious, Pen? That's amazing!"

"I'll be pickin' them up in a few hours. *I have them*, Parsi. Phone records, text messages, emails. There's no getting out of it. No way for them to spin it. They're *cooked*."

"How'd you get all that evidence so fast?"

"It's incredible what you can accomplish when you've got nothin' else goin' on. When you stop daydreamin' and focus on what's real."

"Daydreaming?" He regretted the question instantly, praying to a sleeping god that the conversation wouldn't take an awkward turn.

"You know," she said, Navid able to hear the sudden nervousness in her tone. "Fantasizin'. Thinkin' about stuff you can't have."

"Like, money?" he asked, hoping to steer the conversation in a less uncomfortable direction.

"Yeah, like money, fame...or whatever."

He chewed the inside of his cheek, pacing the floor and spinning his wedding ring around his finger with his thumb. "Well, that's great, Pen. Good work." From the corner of his eye, he saw movement on the laptop's screen. "Hey, Pen, I have to call you back." He ended the call, setting his phone on the counter and bending to look more closely at the computer, reaching for his weapon at the same time.

The cameras showed a man entering the backyard and creeping toward the patio doors. Studying the man's face, he could see immediately that it was Miguel Torres. "Well, color me shocked." Navid moved to the doors, gun pointed as he opened them with his left hand. "Freeze!" he barked, taking Miguel by surprise. "On your knees!"

"Wha--what?" the younger man asked, obviously flustered.

"I won't ask again, mate."

"What's going on?" he asked, slowly crouching down, eyes bulging.

"Hands on your head."

He complied. "What's going on? What's happening?"

"Don't move." He stepped back to retrieve his phone, his eyes fixed on his suspect. He called the police, informing them he had a suspect detained.

"What is this about?" Miguel asked, voice shaking and eyes filling with tears.

"I know what you're here for, mate, and it's not happening. You're under arrest."

"What the fuck?! Since when is being gay in California a crime?"

He blinked. "What?"

"What?"

"You're under arrest for the attempted murder of Ian Berman."

"Huh? You're kidding, right?"

"Do I come off funny to you?"

He put his hands in front of him and started to stand. "Listen,"

"On your knees! I won't repeat myself."

He repositioned himself on the floor. "Okay, okay but I'm telling you, I'm not here to kill Ian. I'm just here to fuck him."

He furrowed his brows. "Against his will?"

"What?! No!"

"Why were you sneakin' 'round the garden if you were here for something consensual?"

"You know his mom, right?"

"Sure," he said, remembering his research. "Gloria Berman, fifty-six. Socialite, fashion designer. What of her?"

"Bro, she's *hardcore* Catholic. It'd kill her if she knew so Ian has a 'girlfriend' and a couple nights a week, I come over and she sleeps in her own room."

"So, you're poly?"

"They are but I'm only interested in Ian."

He looked him over closely, not detecting any signs of deception. Still, he was the only person with motive. "Maybe you want her out of the way. *Maybe* if you can't have him all to yourself, no one will. Is that it? You come to give him an ultimatum? What will you do when he doesn't agree to dump her?"

"I swear, I'm not--" He was cut off by the sharp sound of glass breaking. From upstairs, Poppy screamed.

"Stay there," he commanded, turning and racing to the staircase.

Miguel watched, waited, then bolted out the door.

As Navid took the final step to the landing, he saw Poppy frantically trying to open Ian's bedroom door. "I should've been with him," she squeaked through broken sobs.

"Why aren't you?" he accused.

She stopped, listening through the door and looking up at him with tear-stained cheeks. "It's not my night."

From inside, they heard a strange man shouting, "You're a joke! Look at yourself! You shouldn't have Dad's money. *I should*. It's the least I deserve after that piece of shit sent my mom away, hiding us because he didn't want his career ruined by an affair."

He gulped, questioning his skills as a detective for the first time ever. A half-brother. He had not seen that coming. "Authorities are already on their way," he told Poppy who stood shaking in the hall. "Wait for them outside."

She nodded, hurrying down the steps and out the front door.

Without announcing himself and with one swift kick, he forced the door open, a man with dark hair and eyes standing over Ian, a pistol pointed at his head. Navid's distant cousin was on his knees, hands covering his face and crying.

"Drop it," he ordered, entering the room, eyes glued to the intruder.

"Who the fuck are you?" He took his eyes off his brother but not his weapon.

"Detective Parsi, Scotland Yard. *Drop the weapon.*"

"Fuck you, pig," he said, turning his gun on him and opening fire.

Navid ducked behind the California King-sized bed and returned fire, hitting the stranger in the leg.

"Fuck!" he howled, dropping to the floor. He continued to shoot, dragging himself to the side of the bed, blood smearing across the rug from his gushing wound.

Navid, too, kept firing, eventually landing a shot between the man's eyes, killing him instantly. He'd done it. He'd saved Abel's descendant. He'd fulfilled his mission. The curse he'd been living with for nearly a month, Cain's curse, was finally lifted.

Ian jumped up from his hiding spot next to the nightstand. "Thank you, man," he sputtered. "Seriously, you saved my li--" He stopped, his face falling and going white. "Oh, God."

Navid followed his gaze down to his blood-soaked tee shirt. He'd been hit, three shots to the abdomen. He opened his mouth to speak but no words would come. Only a rattling breath as he fell to his side.

"I'll call an ambulance!" Ian said, dashing out of the room, leaving Navid to die alone for the final time.

Lying on the floor, his body numb and his vision fading, he heard the click of heeled footsteps approaching. Through the fog of imminent death, he could make out a pair of skinny jean-covered legs moving closer. His eyes closed, death's grip around him getting tighter.

Soon, he felt an odd heat warming his stomach and chest. The heat spread through his entire body, every cell, a comforting sensation he'd only felt one other time; when he was saved from the vampires in Petra.

"Gabriel," he whispered, his strength slowly returning as his wounds healed.

"I leave you alone for five minutes and you're already dead again," she admonished. "Fuck, bro, get it together."

His eyes fluttered open, the light of the ceiling fan above her like a halo around her head as she knelt over him. "I," He coughed, sitting himself up and leaning against the bed. "I thought you were back in New York."

"I *was* until I saw a random IG chick's post bragging about how she had a 'hot British cop guarding her man'. I figured you could use some backup." She offered her hand and he took it, letting her yank him up to his feet. "I couldn't let you die for real. Dia would've lost her whole mind and I'd have to deal with B's wrath. He's all happy and shit now but he's just brimming with anger issues looking for an excuse to show themselves and I'm not trying to get my ass electrocuted."

"Is that it, then?" he asked, catching his breath. "Am I back to normal?"

Her eyes bore into his as she "listened". "Yep. Curse broken. Good job, dude." She slapped his shoulder and pulled something from her back pocket. "Take it."

He took the folded paper from her. "What's this?" His eyes grew to saucers as they answered the question for him, a cashier's check in the amount of ten million dollars.

"You have a family, Navid. A kid coming. More after that, I think. Don't go back to work."

"But, I can't just--'

"Be there for them." Her voice was stern, her expression unflinching.

He chewed on his lip, his mind racing.

"I know you hate taking Dia's money so take mine. I have tons."

"Yeah, but--"

"Call it a gift from God."

He chuckled.

"Or just, you know, payment for a job well done."

"Payment?"

"It's the bare minimum I can do. I mean, for real, what do you think it's worth, ending a six thousand-year-old curse on two bloodlines, saving one and redeeming the other? Succeeding in a God-given task? You were already getting into Heaven. This is all I can offer."

He thought it over, Phindi and their family's happiness the only thing left that mattered since Pen had the London corruption case wrapped up. He let out a sigh of acceptance and pocketed the check. "Thank you."

"You feel like paying me back?"

"How could I possibly?"

"I need a favor."

Chapter 19

"Y OU READY?" NAVID ASKED, holding his arm out for Gabriel to take. The two stood at the door of the roof of her apartment building in Manhattan, he in his Italian suit and she in a white and blush ball gown. In front of them lay a pearlescent aisle runner leading through rows of satin-draped chairs to where Wyatt stood waiting, Bible in hand. The guests sat under a canopy of pink and white fairy lights, the setting sun adding to the joyful ambiance.

"You're married," she said, tossing her long, wavy hair over her shoulder, and taking his arm. "Is it hard?"

"Not usually."

As Heart of Mine by Peter Salett began to play, she blew out a nervous breath. "Good enough."

They watched as four-year-old Lucy held her sister, two-year-old Eden's hand, and walked her down the aisle, Valerie's daughters looking precious as flower girls. Next, Michelle pushed baby Tae toward his grandfather who took the rings from a pocket in the front of the pram. When Michelle took her seat next to her husband, parking the pram next to her, Navid and Gabriel slowly began the short walk down the aisle, Gabriel squeezing his bicep so hard, he almost winced. He pat her hand and she released her grip, walking toward her brother who offered a reassuring nod as they approached. Once at the end, they unlinked arms and Navid took his seat next to Allydia.

"You look well," she said quietly.

"I feel better than I have in years," Navid confessed. "Gabriel's healing, no doubt."

"Healing?" She looked him up and down. "When were you hurt?"

Realizing he nor Gabriel had told her what transpired the night before at Ian's place, he decided to lie so as not to upset her on such an important day. "On the way here, I got a bad migraine. She fixed me right up."

"Ah, well, good. I'm glad you're feeling better."

As the song continued to play over the loudspeakers, Poe walked Wendy toward her bride-to-be, the Tituban witch sparkling in a white half-sleeve illusion midi dress with polka dots and lace, her hair piled in a sophisticated bun adorned with pearl encrusted hair-pins. As they reached their destination, Wendy took Gabriel's hands in hers, Poe placing a long ribbon over them before taking her spot next to Wyatt and beginning the hybrid ceremony.

Poe began, "Your paths started separate, have come together, and today we bind you in marriage."

Wyatt opened the Bible to the marked page, looked it over, then tossed it over his shoulder, a twinkle of mischief in his slate gray eyes. The crowd giggled as Gabriel shook her head and smirked. "There's nothing in there you don't already know," he said, giving his sister a wink.

Poe, looking a little flustered, spoke her next practiced line. "Do you promise to celebrate each other's victories?"

Both brides responded, "Yes."

Poe wrapped the ribbon around their clasped hands one time. "Do you promise to support each other through tough times as well as good?"

Again, they responded, "Yes."

She wrapped the ribbon again. "Do you promise to work to see the best in your partner in any circumstance?"

Again, "Yes." Another wrapping.

"And, finally, do you promise to communicate respectfully and with transparency all the days of your lives?"

"Yes," they said, smiling at one another under the twinkling lights as Poe wrapped the ribbon around their hands one final time.

"Blessed be," she said, unwinding and removing the ribbon.

"Blessed be," they responded.

"In the years that I've known you," Wyatt said. "I've seen the ups and downs, watched you break up and get back together. Seen you both die a couple of times and come back."

The wedding guests laughed as did the brides.

"And, through everything, one thing has always been true: you love each other. It's clear as day to everyone who knows you." He looked directly into his sister's eyes as he continued. "This, what you share, you can trust it. I have no doubt that this marriage, this love will last a lifetime."

A small smile appeared on Gabriel's lips. "Thank you," she whispered.

"You're welcome." He handed them one another's rings. "Do you, Wendy, take Gabriel to be your lawfully wedded wife, to love and to cherish, to honor and comfort her, as long as you both shall live?"

"I do," Wendy said, sliding the eternity band on Gabriel's ring finger and giving her hand a squeeze.

"And, do you, Gabriel, take Wendy to be your lawfully wedded wife, to love and to cherish, to honor and comfort her, as long as you both shall live?"

"You, know," Gabriel said, flashing a wide grin and placing Wendy's matching ring on her finger. "I think I do."

"It's about time," he joked. He turned his gaze to the crowd as he announced, "By the power vested in me by the Church of Unity and Togetherness who ordained me via email last week and the state of New York, I now pronounce you partners for life. You may kiss your bride."

With hands clasped, they kissed, the crowd of witches, angels, and former vampires erupting in applause as an instrumental version of Glycerine by Bush played.

"Hey," Will said, tapping Navid on the shoulder, his seat directly behind the detectives.

"Hmm?" He turned to face him.

"How do you know Topher Alexander?"

He rolled his eyes and sighed. "Don't ask."

Navid sat with Will and Michelle's baby while the others danced, happy to get a little practice in before his son arrived. "How did you like the ceremony, Tae?" he cooed, giving the baby's tummy a tickle. "Did you have fun?"

The infant grabbed onto his finger, a small electrical shock buzzing his hand.

"Shit," he yelped, yanking his hand away.

Gabriel sat next to him, laughing as he rubbed his palms together. "He doesn't like being tickled," she told him, giving the baby's cheek a soft pinch.

"I guess not. So, good day."

"Yeah," she said, glancing over at Wendy dancing with Oliver. She stifled a giggle. "Hartley's jealous."

He looked to where the former vampire stood, fists clenched at the sides of her red party dress as she watched them.

"You'd think she would've picked up that the witch isn't interested, what with the wedding and everything."

"She knows. She just can't help it." She crossed her arms and gave him a once-over. "Well, you're miserable."

"I'm not," he asserted. "We're having a great time, aren't we, Tae?"

The baby looked up at him, his expression skeptical.

"I know what'll cheer you up," she said, getting to her feet. "Plus," she gestured to Hartley. "Two birds." She hurried over to whisper something in Wendy's ear. The witch looked over at Navid, politely excused herself, and walked toward him.

"Missing the wife, huh?" she asked as she and Gabriel stood in the aisle next to him.

"Yeah, but I'm all right," he said. "It was a beautiful ceremony, by the way."

"Yeah, yeah," Gabriel said. "Can you do it?"

"I need a picture," Wendy told her.

"Say less." She shoved her hand into Navid's breast pocket and snatched his phone.

"Hey," he protested.

"Shh." She pulled up what she needed and Wendy touched the screen, closing her eyes and saying something in Latin. In a puff of purple smoke, Phindi appeared in the seat next to him, her hand on her swollen belly and a look of shock on her face.

"How did I come to be here?" she asked.

"Uh, magic," Wendy said, smiling broadly. "See ya!" She skipped off, meeting Poe and Charlotte on the dance floor.

Gabriel laughed. "God, isn't she cute as shit? I have no idea how she puts up with me."

"Navid," Phindi said, touching his cheek and kissing him gently. "I've missed you." She looked around at the wedding guests then down at her simple sundress. "I am underdressed."

"You're fine," Gabriel said. "Pretty as a peach." She stared at Phindi's baby bump and again tried to keep herself from laughing.

"What is it?" Navid asked, his heart racing.

"Nothing bad," she assured him. "It's just that you keep arguing about his name."

"So?" Phindi asked, her tone harsh.

"That's normal, innit?" Navid asked.

"Normal, sure. But, kind of dumb."

"Excuse me?" Phindi said, the muscles in her face tightening.

"Don't get your panties in a twist," the angel said. "It's just that he already has a name. It's Cyrus."

"What?" the asked in unison.

She threw her hands up. "I'm just telling you what he told me."

"Fancy a dance?" Wyatt asked, as he strolled over, holding his hand out for his sister to take, which she did.

"Sure."

They made their way to the dance floor, taking a space next to Malik and Valerie who were in their own little world discussing Malik's restaurant, Perry's earning its first Michelin star, and swaying to Bill Wither's classic, Lean On Me.

"Me, too," Gabriel said, hearing her brother's thoughts.

"He would've loved to be here. He liked Wendy, and loved you."

"He loved you, too. Almost more than me."

They both laughed.

"He would've been all, 'This music isn't appropriate for an occasion such as this, sister'," she said in a fake British accent.

"Honestly, sister," Wyatt said, he, too doing his best to sound like Lucifer. "You could have at least walked down the aisle to something a little more classical. Must you always be so yourself?"

They laughed again.

"He's happy at home, though," she said. "When I told him that's where he was going, he almost passed out before Moloch could kill him. I've never felt him that happy. It's good he's there. I miss him, though."

"Me, too."

"May I cut in?" Allydia asked. "I've yet to dance with my husband."

"Of course," Gabriel said, stepping aside. "I'll just be over there gorging myself on chocolate-covered strawberries."

"Have I told you how sexy you look in a tux?" the former vampire queen asked, running her fingertips down his lapels.

"For fuck's sake," Gabriel snapped as she walked off. "Get a room."

Wyatt chuckled as Allydia asked, "Is yours available?"

God's messenger called back, "No!"

"Cyrus, huh?" Navid said, putting his hand on Phindi's bump. "I like it."

"So do I," she said, placing her hand over his. "Ooh." She jumped with the force of the baby's kick.

Navid's eyes lit up. "I guess that settles it, then. Cyrus, it is." He gave his wife a kiss on the cheek.

"Yes." She smiled down at the infant in the pram. "What should we name our next?"

His brows lifted in joyous surprise. "Next?"

"I promised you many. I meant it."

"And, just when were thinking about trying for number two?"

"Well," She thought for a moment. "We'll have to wait the mandatory six weeks, plus it will take some time to find, purchase, and move our things into a new home. Preferably one bigger than the flat in London. How do you feel about New Jersey?"

"New Jersey?"

"Close enough to your family that visiting wouldn't be an issue but far enough that they wouldn't be an annoyance. I hear Howell's nice."

"You're dead set on leaving London?"

"I am dead set on keeping you alive. London is lousy with criminals looking to make names for themselves. Killing the detective who took down an entire gang would be a sure way to rise in the ranks of this gang or the other, wouldn't you agree?"

"I guess."

"So, we'll live here. It's agreed."

He smiled. "Anything to make you happy."

She pecked his lips. "Good." She cringed, rubbing her belly and closing her eyes for a moment. "Because what would make me happy right now is a ride to the hospital."

"The hospital?" He touched her belly again, this time noticing how hard it suddenly felt. "Is it time?"

"It is time."

He jumped from his seat, waving for Will to come over.

"What's up?" he asked before looking down to see Phindi's condition. "Oh. Oh!" The men helped her to her feet, Will taking hold of his son's pram and Navid escorting his wife to the door.

"Cyrus is coming!" Gabriel announced as they passed.

The crowd cheered as the two left the party, on their way to the next adventure.

Also By

The Seventh Day Series – Complete
Read Now on KU
Seraphim
Nephilim
Elohim
Cain
Alukah
Coven
Sinclair

Betrayal of Blood

About Author

Leslie Swartz is an American urban fantasy, dark romance, and horror author. An ex-poet, her writing influences include Shakespeare, Poe, Dickens, Don McLean, and Freddy Mercury. Her works include Betrayal of Blood and award-winning, The Seventh Day Series. When she's not writing, she enjoys reading, spending time with her family and dog, Tilly, and listening to music.

Connect with Leslie
@leslieswartz333
on
Tiktok
Facebook
IG
Threads
Lemon8
And Fanbase